Shadow Walking

Darren Anderson

I Hope You Enjoy
IT!

Shadow Walking

Darren Anderson

ISBN-13: 9-781939-98534-7

For Sarah and Autumn,
my inspiration and my support.

CHAPTER ONE

The moon rises behind a closed mental asylum. A slow drifting shadow begins to drape over the North front of the building, slightly obscuring a young woman with a large carpet bag over her shoulder, approaching the front door. The large, heavy wooden doors of the asylum are pockmarked and warped from negligence and weather. A large sign was loosely tacked to the left door, stating the building was unsafe and condemned for demolition. Beth Vansant stood for a moment, gazing at the sign and began focusing her mind on the task at hand. She reached for the door handle. Of course, it's locked, she thought. Someone might steal the rotted wood. She dropped the bag from her shoulder onto the porch. The bag clanked and rang with the sounds of several items stored within. Beth undid the belt securing the top and reached into it. She emerged with a large crowbar and slammed it into the slight gap that existed between the double doors. Beth struggled, angling the bar to one side when suddenly, an entire piece of the door snapped off and went flying. Beth nearly fell, managing to get her balance at the last second. Well, that worked, just as planned. She pushed open the door and walked into the lobby, placing the bag on the floor she looked over the lobby slowly. It was dark, and it reeked of mildew and rot. A thick coating of dust blanketed the entire lobby like a vast tomb, for some forgotten Pharaoh. Beth thought to herself. It's time to start.

~~~~~

At the South end of the building, a small car had parked. The occupant was dragging various electronic equipment from the trunk and hauling it to the small employee access door. David Jacobson was a small-time ghost hunter/paranormal investigator. He was breaking into the asylum to gather evidence that spirits roamed the halls of the institution. Many people in the small Colorado town had laid several claims that the dead walked the halls, unable to find peace, because of the horrible things they endured before their death. David was determined to capture evidence of any kind. He had brought various recording instruments, thermal and low light cameras as well as motion detectors. David was going to capture actual proof of the afterlife, no matter how long it would take. David approached the employee entrance and immediately smashed the window, so he could reach in and unlock the door. As he reached for the lock, he realized the door was open. Oh, of course, why wouldn't it be open.

Beth had started to pull various items from her carpetbag. Various candles, vials, bottles, a mortar and pestle, small pouches containing herbs and flowers. She placed the candles into a specific geometric pattern. With two larger candles, placed North and South of the epicenter. She proceeds to pour salt around herself, creating a five-foot diameter circle. She pours various plants and powders into the mortar and grinds them down. She adds a potion from one of her bottles and places it upon a small cloth embroidered with a special symbol. She then proceeds to light the candles and mutter an incantation. She repeats a name within her chanting. The name is Asmodeus.

Beth is calling for guidance and assistance to call forth the spirits trapped within the institute. She is there to give them peace and help them move on. She continues to repeat her incantation in an arcane tongue, never rising much above a whisper. Slowly, her words begin to echo from all parts of the lobby. As though her voice was being sent through a concert amplifier. The dust covering every inch of the hall begins to be disturbed, papers swirl as a draft of air whirls all around without any definite source. Soon other voices can be detected, soft at first, but more defined as time goes on. Beth seems to take no notice as she continues her chant. Forms begin to take shape, various people, different ages and backgrounds, all pouring from different corners and attached halls. Then all at once, they stop, and they disappear. An incredibly strong blast of air knocks Beth back and in her mind, what amounts to an angry growl echoes. Beth opens her eyes, she doesn't know who this is, but she now knows why none of these entities have moved on. A certain something is holding them fast.

~~~~~

At the other end of the building, David has set up all his equipment and is doing a system check. Thermal and lowlight cameras are positioned, motion sensors down three halls and lastly, the digital recorders are rolling. David starts to walk around with a flashlight, examining the broken-down structure. He begins to address any beings that may be in the area, hoping to elicit some reaction that he can catch on camera or at least on the recorders. David repeatedly introduces himself and asks if there is anyone around. If anyone wants to talk? Several minutes go by and still there is no response.

Beth abandons the process she started. This is now going to be a fight. Whatever it is holding these spirits, it is doing so to feed on them, to siphon their energy. She grabs another smaller bowl and some different ingredients and assumes a seated position crossing her legs and focuses her mind and begins to chant a new phrase in the same arcane language. The tone is different and its not whispering. She is calling for strength and focusing her energy and driving back the entity. No sooner had she began chanting then something began to take shape a few meters from her. It seemed half here and half in another dimension. Mentally it started to attack Beth. Its goal is to drive her off or damage her mind to bring on insanity. Beth formed a shield around herself. While doing this, she was also focusing on finding what was anchoring the entity here. If she could disrupt its hold on this plane, it will disperse and before it could find a way back, Beth could release the souls trapped within.

~~~~~

Looking slightly defeated, David stood with his flashlight staring at his instruments. There just haven't been any sounds, light orbs, any movement, nothing but a big bust. David thought to himself, this sucks. A few more hours of this and David will likely give up. As David turned to his side to make sure the status light on a motion tracker was still on, a sound drifted gently past him. The hairs on his neck stood at attention. He almost didn't hear it, almost as though his imagination and desire coupled to make him hear what he wanted. Until it sounded again, this time slightly louder. *Help me David.*

David turned back and cried out, "Hello, anyone there?"

Again, the soft voice called, help me David. David started to move toward where the sound seemed to be coming from, but he stopped dead in his tracks. What am I gonna do, how am I gonna help a ghost? If something is hurting a spirit what can I do? All at once a thought popped into his head…. salt. I have salt in the car and a shotgun. The shotgun had been David's grandfathers. It was mixed in with the last bit of items he left for David. David had not yet cleared his car out yet. Putting the last of his Grandfather's stuff into storage felt like burying him all over again, so David kept putting it off. David ran out to the car, popped the trunk and dug for the salt, the rounds and the gun. He pulled a dozen shells out and with his pocketknife cut the plastic housing to dump the birdshot within, so he could reload with salt. He used a bit of duct tape to reseal the case once he filled it with salt. In a few minutes, David had emptied and refilled all 12 and put the shells into his pockets, grabbing the shotgun he ran back into the building to follow the voice. David ran past his instruments and barreled down a hallway.

Beth struggled against the entity; her shield was beginning to crack but she believed she had zeroed in on its connection to this plane. She desperately needed a distraction, something to reduce its onslaught enough for her to use her spell to disrupt its hold. Beth continued to chant to reinforce her shielding and seek guidance for something to help her. Beth called to Asmodeus, but there seemed to be an answer at hand. As she focused her mind and continued her chant, she also slowly reached for a match from her pocket. Beth had to wait for the right moment before igniting the mixture. Sensing she might be up to something else; the entity increased the strength of its attack. At this moment David ran into the lobby from an east hallway. His eyes first fell upon Beth, seated with a bowl in her lap muttering her chants, seemingly staring into space. Then David turned and nearly froze. His eyes fell on something he could scarcely describe or understand. Again, the voice echoed, this time in his head, David help! David snapped out of his fear and struggled to load the salt rounds. As David raised the weapon, the entity became aware of his presence and turned a fiery eye toward him. David once again was frozen, but not from fear this time. The spirit had him. David was locked in a dream state, unable to move or understand what was happening. Beth was now aware of another player on the field. She turned her eyes toward him. Her eyes scanned him and stopped on the shotgun. Beth knew it would be risky, but she changed her focus and disrupted the hold the entity had and shouted one word to him. FIRE. As Beth now received the full brunt of the entities attack and screamed in agony, David awoke from its hold and immediately fired a shot. The salt round struck home and disrupted the entity. The momentary disruption halted the assault on Beth and her mind cleared. She struck a match and dropped it into the bowl that was sitting in her lap. A loud flash popped and Beth yelled out another arcane phrase which led to the entity losing its hold on this plane and disappearing.

Beth rose from her position, picked up the original mortar containing her first mixture and once again began her chant. The spirits arose faster this time and filled the lobby. David stood in awe, still not fully understanding everything that had happened or what was happening now. Beth drew another match from her pocket and lit the mixture. The spirits began to transmute into large orbs of light and then slowly moved from the area, going up and out.

Beth looked relieved and proud and shot a funny look into the air, "cutting your help a little close, don't you think."

David was looking at her and could swear he heard a soft giggle coming from nowhere specific. Beth approached David.

"Thanks for the assist, that salt blast was just the distraction I needed to finish it off." David still looked perplexed, but managed to ask what the entity was?

Beth replied that she was not familiar with that one in particular, but she had seen parasites like that one before. Some kind of small-time, bottom-feeding demon.

"Are there more demons?" David asked.

Beth let out a hearty laugh, "oh more than you can shake a stick at and not all of them are what you would think."

Beth blew out the candles and collected all her equipment. David had been helping her, still asking about what was going on. Beth explained that she was a Witch and was here to release the souls that had been trapped here for so long. She said she might have known something was keeping them here for so long.

"So now you know why I was here and what I do, what were you doing here and how did you just happen to have a shotgun loaded with salt?"

David explained he was an amateur ghost chaser, even had a card which he shakily brought out of his wallet. The adrenaline was still coursing through his veins, a bit.

"I investigate hauntings, monster rumors, whatever. As far as the salt, the idea just sort of popped into my head to go get it. But to be honest, this is the first real thing that has ever happened to me."

The whole time Beth was looking him over, staring intently into his eyes. When David was done explaining why he had been there, Beth smiled and said, "yup, you will do just fine."

David laughed and said, "okay, wait what, do for what? Where are you going?"

"Go get your equipment David, and pull the car around, we have things to discuss."

"Wait, who told you my name?"

"Who indeed," Beth replied.

CHAPTER TWO

Beth decided that she should start working together with David. She felt that Asmodeus had sent him to her, so she wasn't going to turn him aside or ignore the importance he may have in her life. Some of their first endeavors together involved hauntings. This one involved an entity that was terrorizing a family. It was focused on the Mother of the family primarily, but everyone was suffering. The Spirit was that of a maligned individual. The attacks were subtle at first but have become more violent, mostly directed toward the wife and mother of the home. She had suffered a dislocated shoulder from the last encounter and the multiple hospital trips are starting to draw legal attention.

David had researched the history of the home and found the

former Mildred Wrencrest. She was an abhorrent person. She actively frightened children, stirred discontent with neighbors and though it was never proven, had likely poisoned local dogs, along with being just a miserable excuse for a human being. David decided Mildred was the likely haunter. She was a mean, cold and likely disturbed person in life and would seem to be no better in death. She had died 60 years ago and the family had moved into her former house on the anniversary of her death. Something that was celebrated by the neighborhood. The focus of her malice on the Mother would seem to be because in life, Mildred was alone, unappealing to most male suitors and rumor had it that Mildred was barren. Unable to be a mother and unable to keep a man, she seemed to be focusing her hate and envy on a woman who seemed to have everything Mildred could not.

Flashing to the house, Beth had been attempting to reason with Mildred. The family had been asked to move out and visit relatives for a few days. So far Mildred was refusing to cooperate. She had tried simple scares already, moving objects, breaking mirrors, but when she flung a large vase at Beth's head, that was the final insult.

Looking rather cross, the Witch proclaimed, "You want it rough, fine, rough it is! Could have been pleasant, could have walked you into the next plane, but no... you must be a raging bitch. Well, now it's my turn."

Beth walked over and picked up her large carpetbag and dived in immediately. She rose from it with a familiar mortar and pestle, along with a few varied bags and a large box of matches. She set the ingredients down, tore into the first bag and began to grind and crush the herbs. Without missing a beat, she grabbed another bag and jukes her head to left as a lamp just missed her. Mildred was getting more and more aggressive. A familiar entity slightly emerged, it wanted to watch the show. Unlike before, Beth was very much aware of its presence, but due to circumstances, she was unable to address it properly. Beth moved faster, grinding and mixing and chanting some arcane incantation under her breath. The Witch grabbed a match and ignited the concoction just as the entity manifested in all its glory to make a full-on assault. As the match hit the contents, a pungent smoke billowed out of the bowl along with some vibrant, colorful lights and Beth blew the smoke directly at the oncoming Mildred. The smoke encompassed her and a horrid scream shattered some of the glass and crystal cups in the kitchen as the entity seemed to completely be dissolved into nothingness.

"You lived a horrible life, you died unmourned. Now you have been painfully excised from this plane of existence. I hope this opened your eyes to other ways of being, but whether or not you embrace a change, you are done hurting these people," Beth shifted her focus to the new participant, "so, did you enjoy the show or are you waiting for your turn?"

A soft but reverberating voice spoke. "I did indeed enjoy it. Why though, I wonder, did you waste your time trying to discuss things?"

Beth declared every living being deserves a chance at redemption. Even a highly unpleasant one.

"Now I have a question, you seem familiar to me, though you are working hard to hide from me. So... who are you?" The being let out a small laugh.

"For now, simply an interested party... your companion is here." With that, the being departed, leaving Beth mildly perplexed.

A moment later David arrived.

"So, did everything go smoothly? Was my intel correct?" Beth breathed a deep sigh and looked over her shoulder towards him.

"Smoothly, not so much, your intel was spot on and the entity has been handled. Feel free to call the family and tell them..." Before Beth could finish her thought, David interrupted with, "This house is clean!!!"

Beth rolled her eyes and proceeded to pack up her bag.

David stood looking at her. "What?? That was funny!!"

She arched her right eyebrow but did not stop packing or even look his way, but she did slightly smile. His dumb jokes and goofy bravado were welcome. David kept things in perspective and he kept her grounded. He helped offset the sense of having the world on her shoulders. David had spiritual Teflon, very little of what they encountered stuck to him. His moral was almost unshakable and that positivity is contagious and welcome. Kind of like a big, dumb puppy. That thought made her laugh out loud just a bit.

When everything was brought out to the car, Beth turned to him and asked about their next case.

"Well, we are actually, without a case. I figured you could use a break anyway, after this pain in the ass."

Maybe go home and see that special lady...before the Moon comes anyway. That was a great idea.

Beth was a bit tired. This cleansing was her third one in the last four weeks and before that, David had to take down a vampire who was praying on Homeless Teens. Beth did not like him going on his own...spiritual Teflon or not, David on a solo mission wore on her mind more than any spiritual cleansing. So, it was a relief to have him back where she could keep an eye on him. So, it had been a very busy month or so. The house clearings generated some revenue, so that was a plus, but it was still very draining to do battle with so many angry and resistant spirits. Especially when not one of them was willing to take the easy path. Add the stress over David and she was completely exhausted.

David dropped Beth off at her place. It was a modest home in rural Boulder, Colorado. The home was on a nice piece of property, three acres she had inherited from an Aunt years ago, that butted right next to Rocky Mountain National Park. This meant that for several miles in any direction, she had no neighbors. This was perfect for her. People could be taxing. Being a Witch and empathic, made her sensitive. Her inability to shut out others' negative energies made existing around them…difficult. So many voices, so much going on, it was hard to relax when you must constantly focus on blocking so much out. Being out here, meant she didn't have to. Beth could drop her focus and unwind. Of course, there was another reason for this, her lover.

Brianne Larson was a vibrant woman, very much a people person. That person that is always the life of the party, the one everyone gravitates towards. That person people are drawn to and attracted to. Beth's lover was every bit this kind of person. She worked as a game designer and tester for Blizzard Entertainment. This allowed her extremely flexible hours and the ability to work from home. She had every nerds' dream for a workroom. Huge monitors, several game systems and computers so amped up they nearly defy description. Brianne was also one more thing, 3 days of every month, she was a monster. The Witch's lover was, in fact, a Werewolf.

Beth researched lore and Brianne's personal family line for a process or even a ritual that would grant her control. It is very possible that in time, her lover may learn to control it herself. Most of the lore on Werewolves pertains to killing them or creating them, even curing them. But there is very little about their society, their normal habits or history. Why doesn't she just cure her? That is the thought Beth figures would jump into anyone's mind. The thing is, her lover revels in it. It makes her strong, confident and gives her a special sense of belonging to the world around her. Brianne feels so connected and so long as they live away from people, there is nearly no chance of anyone running afoul of her alter ego. Beth loves that about her, it brings them together and creates a connection that few people could ever even imagine, let alone have in this life. Plus, Beth can connect to and influence her even under the chaos of animalistic urges. So, no matter what, Beth is never in real danger from her lover.

Beth walked in to find her Lover hard at work and by work she meant playing video games. She walked over to her, sat right next to her on the floor and gently laid her head on her lover's shoulder. Beth sat there and took in the scent, the warmth and the aura of her lover. As she leaned deeper against her, she felt her lean back into her and laid her head onto hers.

"You seem tired Babe, are you okay? Did something go wrong?" Another deep sigh escaped Beth and she responded with a slight no.

"Nothing wrong, just a little trouble. I handled it, it's done, how are you?"

"Me? I am getting pissed about this game. I cannot seem to rectify this damn glitch!! Mother Fucking, Cunt Sucking Slutterang character will not do what I need him to do! Arg!" Beth loved her flamboyance; how verbally passionate she is.

"Maybe you need to unplug for a few and sit with me and have dinner." The Witch whispered in her ear.

The game was paused and the two of them withdrew to the couch and wrapped their arms around each other. Tightly entwined, eyes shut, smiles upon their faces.

Brianne said, "whose turn to cook is it?"

"Umm that would be yours."

"So, Pizza?" Beth smiled deeply but opened her eyes just wide enough to roll them.

"Yah, no, we have to pay extra to get them to come way out here. Worth It!" Her lover proclaimed.

The call made, the television set up for a movie marathon and the two of them snuggled into each other.

The next morning Beth awoke to her cell phone ringing. She reached for her phone, struggling against her lover's arm, who tightened her grip the moment she stirred. Finally reaching the phone, after it stopped ringing, she saw David's number. She re-dialed him, he answered in a slightly panicked state.

"Hey, hey where are you??? There is some serious trouble!"

"I am at home, I'm in bed, what trouble, what's wrong, you sound off?"

"I ran into some people, they wanted to hire us, really interested in you, too interested in you. I told them I had to check on something, check our calendar, etc. They followed me...I think they thought I was going to you. I went to the office and slipped out the back and took my car."

"Why do you think they wanted me, what was off?"

"Too many questions, about your background, your strengths, what you can do, who you trained under, who you pray to, disciplines, yadda, yadda, yadda. I know when someone is pumping me for info and when someone just wants to know if we are professional. These guys are bad news in some way." Beth looked very puzzled.

"Look, give me a few and I can meet you somewhere." Beth said.

"That would be great, why don't we hit Delilah's Diner...I could eat."

Beth got herself together and headed out to D's. Pulling in, she saw David's car in the parking lot. She parked, walked in and looked for him. Something seemed off. She knew he was worried, but there was something else. She couldn't quite put her finger on it as she walked to his booth. Then as she sat, it hit her. The aura around him, it's off, he had been glamoured...it's in his eyes. Beth immediately reached into her bag, looking for something to break the spell when the person in the booth behind her struck her with something that felt like lightning and then all went black.

David awoke from the spell and found himself tied up to a chair. Everything was blurry at first and then came into focus, he knew this place. Its Beth's house, been there a few times. There was something else, someone was in the room with him. It's her Lover. Brianne was also just coming clear. She raised her head and called out to Beth. As she looked around, she saw David and immediately she panicked.

"What are you doing here?? You can't be here, not now!" It was already night.

The moon had risen and, in a few moments, Brianne would begin to change and without Beth's presence to calm her, she would likely tear David apart.

Beth also began to come clear. Her eyes were blurry, but things came into focus. She was tied to wood. It seemed to be in an 'x' shape with her wrists and ankles tied to each end of the 'x'.

"Oh Christ, ya gotta be kidding me." She blurted out.

Around her were about a dozen people in bronze robes with red accents. They were chanting and seemingly blessing an extremely large knife. Apparently, I am going to be sacrificed. The main priestess stopped, looked toward Beth and smiled.

"You are exceptionally gifted in your connection to the world and what is beyond. We wish to partake in that power. Unfortunately, we need something from you to accomplish this, something we didn't figure you would just hand over to us.... your pretty little heart."

Beth sent a stern look toward the priestess, then closed her eyes as if focusing on some other issue. The group returned to chanting and to the preparations for the ceremony. The full moon must be at its apex before the sacrifice can happen. Within her mind, Beth could hear that same soft voice return to her.

"A bit of an issue, wouldn't you say?" Upon speaking to her, the being allowed itself to be revealed to her.

"Asmodeus, you are the one who has been watching lately? Why be so coy, why hide?"

"Oh, I have been watching you for much longer, but lately

you have become much more interesting, I didn't want to influence what had happened.... your partner seems fun."

At that moment Beth realized David was not around, was he dead, was he safe, where was he? Panic began to wash over her, she then immediately calmed her mind, panicking will not help anyone.

Asmodeus whispered again to her, "perhaps your partner could use a nudge in the right direction."

Meanwhile David told Brianne to hurry and untie him, so he could getaway! The lover struggled and got through most of the bindings when a wave of pain struck her. The change has started. The stress of the situation and not knowing what had happened to Beth pushed the change ahead of schedule. Brianne called out to David, told him to hurry while she tried to suppress the change. David frantically struggled against the ropes, he twisted and writhed when suddenly, he was able to slip out and unravel them. All at once, a voice came into his head. Beth had reached him. She urged him to find her fast. David was finally free from the ropes and ran outside. There he realized his car was missing and he had no weapons to fight with. What was he to do?

Beth had been focusing on David to guide him, she had been ignoring the fact that the assembly was almost ready to start cutting. They approached her, when she snapped out of her trance.

"Nice of you to come back to us, just in time to witness your own demise." The priestess mused.

Darren Anderson

Beth spoke up, "so, before I become the sacrifice of the week, any chance of you folks wanna tell me what order or group you are from, for curiosity sake?" The Priestess looked and smiled at Beth and then replied.

"Does the image of a bronze bull and flames reveal anything to you?" Before Beth could respond David crashed through the bushes that were surrounding their site.

It was not far from the house, they had set it up in the woods just beyond, after they had put a spell on David and had him lead them all around their property. The group turned to face him.

"So, you came out of the spell and thought you were gonna single-handedly fight all of us and save your friend? I think you overestimate your abilities, for your arrogance, we will put that spell back on you and have you sacrifice yourself to our Lord."

David, who was slightly out of breath and was bleeding a bit from wounds on his arm. They looked like knife cuts, more than scrapes from the bushes.

David looked at the priestess and said, "oh, I am not here to fight you, I am actually the rabbit and the distraction."

"Rabbit, distraction? What the hell are you talk..." Before the priestess could finish her thought, Brianne crashed through the bushes, just to the right of David's position.

She was huge, shaggy, muscular and her eyes burned with a serious rage. As she turned toward David and looked him over, she quickly turned right towards the group and lunged with a speed and ferocity seldom seen in life. Half of them were slashed with deep claw marks in the first few seconds. The rest attempted to run but did not get far. David ran to Beth and cut her down, with the same pocketknife he cut himself with, to lure her lover to follow him. He noticed that her eyes looked off and she was not actually seeing him now.

"Who or what are you looking at, because I get the feeling it isn't me?" Beth asks.

"Didn't you wonder why she didn't attack you immediately upon arriving?"

"Ahh…you're working on her…arent you?"

"Working on her? No, influencing her, a bit. She is about done now. They apparently never probed your mind about your lady, or they might have brought something to deal with her." David remarked.

"Oh no, they knew. That is why they left you in the room with her, tied to a chair. What they didn't know is how much influence I have over her or that you would be able to slip the knots and lead her here." Beth stated.

"Sometimes I can come up with a good idea or two. Especially when I am about to get killed!"

"I was surprised I was able to beat her here; the change must have taken longer than normal." David said in a surprised tone.

Beth looked at David, then towards Brianne's direction, "yah, lucky, she was a little slow." Beth laughed to herself a little.

The two gathered the remains of the group, checked their IDs, got anything useful from them and then piled them into a rather large funeral pyre. Beth used a special concoction, then set them ablaze. The ingredients she used along with the incantation would ensure nothing would be left to lead anyone to her, Brianne or David. Brianne was busy running free, trying to burn off her rather large meal. Beth was left to ponder Asmodeus' interaction in their lives. She reasoned that Asmodeus helped David slip his ropes.

"So, are you just being playful, or do you have something deeper in mind?" Beth said to herself.

CHAPTER THREE

A week later David and Beth were in a small office's backroom, watching David as he was concentrating on his experiment.

Beth sarcastically spoke, up the musical scale, "that is not gonna work, you are gonna get messed up," as she smiled.

"Look you, you know all the Hoo-Doo, mystical stuff...this, this is science, I got this!" David gruffly said, without taking his eyes off his contraption.

Hoo-Doo, really? That is what you are going with? That Hoo-Doo has saved your ass a few times, so, a little respect please."

"Um, yeah, sorry. So, anyway, ghosts are essentially energy, focused, powerful, but a form of energy. This baby, once it's been adjusted, will disrupt their energy patterns or signature, then

POOF temporary displacement of the troublesome soul!!"

"You're going to die down there." Beth made her best Red Queen impression.

"Oh My God, you are so funny." In his best Valley Girl impression.

"Look, it's basically just a portable Electromagnetic Pulse device."

"Well, can we agree to try a simple situation first and not some full-on, Hell sent spirit that could tear a house apart?" Beth said very seriously.

Beth was very worried about this situation, she did not want to tell David, but she was very worried. David was a good friend and to her almost a kid, or a puppy, either way she was not happy with his idea.

"What kind of spirit did you have in mind?" David asked.

"Casper." She smiled very brightly.

He was scowling at her, but he did not respond.

"I just mean, let's ease into this ordeal. You have some serious weapons and skills, why do you need this electronic monkey wrench?" Beth's concern was coming out more in her voice.

"Okay, first, there is always room to improve and to expand one's repertoire. Second, how dare you! Electronic monkey wrench?"

"You are just jealous; you don't have my creative flare." Beth without missing a beat.

"Or an inheritance burning a hole in your wallet." "Don't

press me woman!" David jokingly snapped. Satisfied with himself, he turned back to finish his project, determined it would work.

It was time to put his project into action, a week later ready to prove himself, both found themselves on their next job in a dilapidated home, several years old. Beth was looking slightly impatient.

"Do we have an ETA on your masterpiece's debut? Or will we be using it on ourselves, because we have already dropped dead?"

The Hunters' eyes were focused on his contraption, a couple minor sparks flared. The back of the machine was open and wires were sticking out in several directions.

"Don't rush me, these are delicate, sensitive materials."

Rolling her eyes, while she waited down a side hallway, where objects were being violently disturbed.

"Yeah, well, if you don't hurry up, your delicate materials are gonna get thrashed." Down the hall, the entity was manifesting.

Casper, it was not, "do I need to get my ingredients ready or what? Seriously, this one has some bad vibes just pouring out of it. I don't know who it used to be, but it is not the librarian that owned this place and supposedly died here."

David frantically worked as the entity, in full form, was barreling down. It was looking half-human and half reptilian. Its eyes looked empty and its teeth, huge. It had a blue hue and was still wispy and translucent in places and was flying right toward the duo. Suddenly it vanished. The whole place went quiet.

Beth's eyes widened, she immediately went for her tools and materials. It was too late, the entity manifested right between them. In a blink David and his glorious contraption were flung across the room and crashed into a dilapidated table, which crumbled on impact. His shoulder dislocated and his left hand broke at the knuckles. The shock of David flying freestyle across the room ruined her focus and the entity swiped at Beth. The touch of the malevolent creature burned her chest as if she had been dipped into some intensely cold concoction. Beth staggered back from the strike and regained composure. She focused her mind and recited a quick spell that disrupted the entity.

Beth however was no longer holding her tools of the trade; they were spread all over the floor and she would need a minute to gather and reorganize. A minute she no longer had. The entity had already recovered from the spell and moved even faster than before. At the last moment David rose to his knees from the floor, leveled off his contraption and yelled Gotcha! He flipped a switch and turned a sort of crank. The contraption opened at the front, revealing a reflector dish and a focusing aperture and huge pulse of light and loud buzz erupted. The discharge went right at the entity, which stopped it right in its would-be tracks. An unearthly noise arose from within it, then windows shattered and in a moment, it violently shimmered out of this plane of existence.

"Ha! that's right, suck it!" David was celebrating rather loudly while still on the floor.

He was bleeding from the mouth and was noticeably hurt. Beth was quiet, her eyes wide, she was just a little stunned. She had never seen any piece of modern technology ever have any effective use in their rarified field of endeavor.

Finally. She spoke, "holy shit. I really didn't think that was gonna do a damn thing besides put on a light show and maybe screw up our cell phones."

"Once I got the kinks out, it worked great!"

Great...Seriously? That was too close, that entity was much more powerful and aggressive than it was supposed to be." Beth was fuming at this point.

"What the fuck happened to the librarian?" David turned to Beth.

"The only thing I could find about this place said it was a librarian who owned the house and died here. She was a quiet, kind lady, that no one had any complaints about." David responded.

"Obviously, someone else moved in. Probably drove the librarian out. If the Librarian was ever here in the first place. Or maybe she was not what everyone thought she was. Either way, you rushed the research, just to put on your laser light show!" Beth interjected, "that was poor thinking, dick-jacket!"

David tried to calm her, "okay, okay, I may have done a superficial exploration, but it turned out okay, right?"

Now the Witch was looking at him with a significant scowl,

"no more rush jobs, agreed? Look at you, you were beaten to hell, that is not good! This could have really gone south!" Beth was looking particularly pissed.

David with tail tucked, "okay, okay, yes, no more half-assing it. I was a little excited, I won't do that again. Are we good?" David said sheepishly.

"I am fantastic, you are an idiot, dick-jacket, but yes we are good." Something about David's level of enthusiasm bothered Beth.

It reminded her of someone, Alicia, of course. Maybe bringing David into this was a mistake. That was still cool though, you gotta admit! David and his never-ending enthusiasm. It was grinding Beth's gears, partly because of an old worry and partly because it made her want to smile, despite her anger.

"I will compliment you later, after the idea of nearly being pooched wears off."

David interjected, "oh, can you not tell Brianne about this…least not till after the full moon?" Hazaahh, reality finally sunk in! Beth then just busts out into laughter as they walked away.

Chapter Four

In their slightly rundown, but still professional looking office, David and Beth were busy working. The sign on the door leading to the street read Metaphysic Investigations. While the team was in the process of moving in more supplies, they were also doing some preparatory work. Beth was itemizing ingredients and making sure her travel bag has a little of this and a little of that to ensure most situations could be handled. David was pouring through lore books, many tomes purchased over a long lifetime by his Grandfather and passed on to him, along with several texts Beth brought to the mix. David was slightly humming to himself as he transfers pertinent information to a quick reference book, a log for easy access on how to deal with all manner of creatures. As David scribbled faster, the Humming increased in volume. It became apparent that he was recreating "Mexican Radio" by Wall of VooDoo.

After several minutes, Beth called out, "can we change the station! Cause that CD is stuck!"

With a ruffled brow, David looked up from the pages and books, the tune had temporarily stopped. Beth smiled, but did not look at his perplexed face. After a moment or two, the head dropped back to the pages and the tune restarted. When does the request line open? His head did not move, but his eyes roll-up. Point taken. A remote is searched for, discovered and used to start a stereo sitting on a small end table. An alternative station began to blare some modern rock band's anthem.

"Thank you!" Echoed from the other side of the shelves.

A mocking, "What-ever!", was fired back.

"Hey, how are we able to have an office, anyway?" Beth asks, "I mean, we don't really charge much for working out situations."

"I mean, I have my own business, but it only covers some bills and allows me to put away a little for retirement."

"The wife covers the rest and then some."

"And while we are talking about work, you don't seem to have a job, outside of this stuff, so how are we affording this *luxurious* base of operations?"

"I know I have explained this, but once more for the cheap seats. I have a modest inheritance."

"I am not going to be buying my own island anytime soon,

but I have a good nest egg. My Grandfather did well with real-estate and some better investments plus he also left me a few items I can sell if needs arise. Roll it all together and I do not need a *regular* job for financial needs."

"Really? So what kind of items do you have to sell?

"Well, if you must know, I have in mint condition, Captain America #1, Marvel Comics #1 and the granddaddy of them all, Detective Comics #27, the introduction of Batman!" David said in a deep gravelly voice, "all I gotta do is go online, find the right buyer site and I will have almost 2 million! I also have a few other items as well, but barring any huge costs, I will never have to touch a single item. Thanks Granddad!"

Beth's eyes grew like an anime girl's, "well, I guess we are gonna be okay for quite a while."

David walked over, a huge smile on his face. "Look, aside from this office and a few pieces of technology, we don't have a lot of expenses. Some herbs, a little silver now and then and some slightly rare plants, nothing too overly costly. Plus, I purchased the whole building, which comes with an apartment above the office and I have already moved in!"

Beth started to say something congenial, then stopped herself.

"Wait, you did what? I thought you had a place, a nice little house?"

"Had, being the keyword. I sold it, that being the other reason we are good for a while financially. I had a few acres and a modest house, that covered buying the whole office building, instead of just renting space."

Beth rolled her eyes a bit and retorted, "fine, but the first time you walk down here in slippers and underwear and nothing else, I am gone!"

David busted out laughing and held up 3 fingers, boy scout-swearing to never do that.

As the two went back to work, the retro-looking landline rings. The two-stop dead in their tracks as the phone continues to ring. They are dumbfounded and after the 5th ring David, snapped out of his daze, dived for the phone.

"Metaphysic Investigations, David Jacobson speaking, how may I help you? Uh-huh, MmmHmmm, Yeah...okay sure."

David hung up the phone. Beth looked at him with impatience.

"Well?" Beth asked. "Oh, that was the plumber checking in about the room above, I had a leaky faucet."

"Schmuck."

David sat with a, *proud of himself,* smile upon his face. Beth had a face that would seem to suggest contemplation of violence. Before anything could happen, the phone rang again. Beth lunged, but was too slow, as David scooped the receiver up!

"Metaphysic Investigations, David Jacobson, speaking, how may I help you?"

There was a woman on the other end of the line. She was asking him if they were serious about investigating weird things, out of the ordinary things, things science could not readily explain. She began to say that a friend of hers went hiking, then went missing. Later her remains were found, mutilated almost beyond recognition. The Forest Service and Police both said it was a bear. She was not buying that. Her name was Mary Parker and she just happened to be a wildlife biologist. Mary specialized in the mammals of North America. She was quite familiar with bear attacks and the kinds of damage they would inflict as well as how much they will likely consume, if at all. The Police and Forest Service reps were mistaken, the Pathologist was mistaken, or they were covering up something.

"Look, I know bear attacks, I know most animal attacks, how they attack, what they eat, what their claw marks are like, even what their teeth impressions are like. At the risk of sounding a bit dramatic, this was no animal that naturally exists on the North American Continent. I don't know what this was, but it was not natural." David's face was stern, the more she spoke, the more serious his face got.

Beth stood by and felt the tension through the phone, this was not the plumber. This was a serious case. Once David got all the contact information and location of the attack, he started to research other attacks in the area that matched the report. There seemed to be a pattern, for that area. Every winter there are hikers that go missing and some are found later, mutilated and mostly consumed in the same way as this new victim. Most of the victims are consumed, but there is no evidence of scavengers feeding on the scraps. There only seems to be one animal having fed, yet there is an inordinate amount of tissue consumed, too much for just one animal. Even a grizzly does not eat this much, especially not in one sitting. The experts say the victims must have been fed upon over a prolonged amount of time, however the pathology report does not support that idea. The more David researched and relayed information, the more worried Beth became.

David piped up, "I don't think this is any kind of Lycanthrope, Vamps don't eat a body and the feeding is too fresh for Ghouls and other types of Revenants. Though a Lamia could eat that much in one sitting, they are not usually found in this country, nor do they come back to the same place every winter. Information only goes back so far, being such a remote area, but there is a pattern, a cycle. I am missing something, must be something having to do with the region maybe?"

Beth spoke up, "try doing a crossover with Algonquin Tribal Lore."

David looked up Algonquin.... "why does that sound familiar? Oh shit...Wendigo?"

Beth looking worried. "Give the man a cigar, that is likely our critter."

Immediately David dug for his tribal lore tomes, "okay, so how do we waste a Wendigo? Whisp, Weather...Wendigo! Okay, here we go...uhh...silver, salt, fire and a good cleansing spell to remove a curse.

Beth piped up, "I am not a huge fan of dealing with flesh and blood problems, I am much better with spirits and demons."

Shadow Walking

David swung round in his chair, pulling up a shotgun.

"That's okay, I got the physical aspects handled. One 12-gauge shotgun, loaded with silver buckshot, a silver knife, plenty of salt, gasoline and a nice big box of Ohio Blue Tip Matches! I will leave the spell casting and curse cleansing to the expert!"

"Well aren't you the sweet one." Beth sarcastically uttered.

David got slightly serious again, "now these things are supposed to be very fast and terrific hunters and they mostly come at night...mostly."

"Please stop." Beth said smiling.

"So anyway, I think we need to recon the hunting grounds during the day and set up some traps. We are also gonna need some bait, so before we head out, I am gonna need to give up a pint or two of blood, they don't seem to go for anything besides human meat."

"Oh goodie, I will get the juice and cookies for you and the needle and bags. Lucky for you, I have had to learn to be an amateur nurse, thanks to my Werewolf wife."

After some shopping for extra materials such as blood bags, needles, etc and a cooler for the blood that can go on a plane, David worked on booking a flight to Hibbing, Minnesota. Then he set up a car rental, so they could drive up to Ely, the closest city to the area where the incidents had been happening. After booking everything, David relayed that he was gonna ship the trapping equipment and some other items express delivery, so they wouldn't have to explain the contents to airport security.

The items would be waiting for them at the Silver Rapids Inn. They would fly out in a few days, with a reservation at the Inn, in Ely.

The duo arrived at Hibbing, grabbed their luggage and checked out the rental shop for a ride to get them to Ely. There were several modern, gas-friendly, hybridized vehicles for rent. The two were spending entirely too much time checking out the rides, almost as though this was the reason, they came to Minnesota in the first place. Finally, at the back of the yard, they found it, an old Volkswagen Bus. The two stopped in their tracks, their eyes widened and their jaws dropped. This was it; this is what they needed.

The rental rep stood behind them with a confused look on his face, "Are you sure you wouldn't rather try one of our economy rides? I am not sure if this is even still on the rental books."

"Well, how much if we just buy it?" Asked Beth, with a large smile.

About $8000.00 dollars later the two rolled out in their powder blue Volkswagen Bus. Their own Mystery Machine, that is what they had thought as soon as they saw it.

"Oh shit, I guess I need to cancel our return flight." Worth it.

A couple hours later and the team was pulling into Ely, Minnesota. Their hotel was in sight. The Silver Rapids Inn, a rustic design, not unexpected for the part of Minnesota they were in. Not far from the Canadian border and close to the wilderness. They checked in at the front desk.

Shadow Walking

The clerk came from the back office, "Can I help you folks?"

"Checking in, please." David replied.

"Just a king bed then?" The desk clerk asked.

Immediately Beth burst out in giggles, while David turned with a slightly annoyed look on his face.

"I am not sure I see the humor; I would make a great catch!"

"Perhaps, but not for me, 2 queens please." The clerk was looking confused and a little embarrassed but selected a key and had them sign their registry card.

"Here ya are, 2 keys, 2 queen beds, room 235. The elevator is just around the corner, you folks have a good afternoon."

"Thank you, we will. Oh, I was expecting a package, has it arrived yet?"

"Hold on a moment and I will check. Oh yes, we have a large package with your name on it, did you want this now?"

"If it's okay, can I pick it up in the morning?"

"That would be just fine, sir." As the two walked away there were more mumblings and giggles down the hall.

"I figured we could grab something to eat, call Mary and set up a time and place to meet, so she can show us to the area where her friend went missing and where the remains were found. I will grab our package in the morning after breakfast, the sign on the desk said they have a nice little restaurant across from the lobby, opens at 7am. After Mary shows us around, we need to decide on the best way to lay the traps and the bait, also find where we are gonna be." David explained.

"Oh yes, that is very important, we need to find a place we can have time to react if it's as fast as lore would seem to imply." Beth added.

Maybe a small cave or a group of trees to give us a height advantage...the high ground and all? We will use the blood to bait it, the traps to slow it and I will do the blasting with the silver," David explained, "After that, you do the cleansing.

Beth spoke up, "You sound like you have this worked out, how about I sleep in and you call me when you need the counter curse work done?"

"First of all, no. Second of all, I could really use an extra set of eyes and someone who can feel when something supernatural is approaching without even seeing it. Grandpa taught me a lot about tracking and hunting, but this is slightly different. You would be a great early warning system." David noticed Beth's look of concern.

"We are gonna be fine, this will work out." David remarked.

"Oh yes, you know this from all the other Wendigos you have hunted and killed? I have never even seen one, only read the lore, I am guessing the same goes with you. That makes me a little nervous, this is new territory."

David tried to be reassuring, "All true, but you do have a Werewolf for a wife, that's close, she is pretty fierce and..." David is cut off in mid-thought.

"My wife is nothing like this thing, she is natural, she is not a curse or mutation or disruption of nature! She is an animal, yes, but that is where the comparison ends. I have a connection with her, a bond that transcends what she is! Even at her worst, she could never be anything close to what this is, she is still who she is, even when changed ...or do you really think you outran her in the woods, especially all jacked up? She did not chase you, she followed you, she followed you to get to me." Her face was stern, like some relief carved out of granite as a warning to others.

There was a slight glow behind her eyes that shone like a blaze but had begun to diminish as her composure was regained. He stood there for a moment, watching her calm down, waiting for the right moment to apologize.

"I'm sorry, I didn't mean to say she was." Again, he was cut off in mid-thought.

"It's okay, I am still sensitive, protective of her. I know what you meant, I know it wasn't meant to demean her, I am worried and tired, this is out of my wheelhouse and it's got me agitated."

David interrupted this time, "We both need to relax and get some rest, we will start tomorrow."

They had a good meal and got some rest as best as possible. The two of them laid in bed for a bit, running through the next day in their heads. This was not going to be a ghost hunt. This thing is flesh and blood, incredibly strong and fast and has only one goal, feast on human flesh. It cannot be reasoned with, begged off or bribed. It won't care about anything you have to say or who you will leave behind or any other sympathy card a person can throw. A Wendigo is a monster in the truest sense of the word and in a day, they will likely face one.

The two snapped up to the wakeup call that David had set the night before. After answering it, he ran into the bathroom figuring he can get his morning rituals done faster and leave the rest of the morning to his compatriot. Only one eye was visible of hers as he grabbed his stuff and darted into the bathroom.

"Rise and shine, Muffin!" He bellowed from within the bathroom and then began to sing a familiar tune.

She recoiled from the noise and buried herself deeper into her blankets and sheets.

"You are a monster!" She shrieked back at him.

Once all the pleasantries were over, they went down for a nice breakfast, heavy on the bacon with coffee and orange juice. They then moved their gear into the Scooby bus and David went back and signed for his package. Taking it out to the bus, he opened it to make sure all the materials were intact. The next step was to call Mary and set up a time and place to meet.

"Hello Mary, yes we are here, we are at the Silver Rapids Inn, where can we meet?"

"I know exactly where you are, I will meet you at your hotel's parking lot and take you to where the incident occurred." Mary told David.

Around 20 minutes later, a Ford pickup showed up and a small blonde got out of the cab. She was just over five feet, blonde, jaw-length hair and glasses. She walked up quickly and confidently.

"So, you are the ones, huh? I really hope you can help, there is something out there and it is not right."

David piped up, "No worries Mary, we handle this kind of thing all the time, all the time!"

Beth shifted her eyes and deep under her breath said, "Really, dude...Ghostbusters?"

He just looked at her and smiled a goofy grin, "So, lets head out to the site."

After about a 40-minute drive, the last leg of which was over something that was more of a path and way less of a road, they arrived at their destination. They all exited their vehicles and approached a trail.

Mary spoke up, "It's on foot from here, about another couple miles in at least."

"I will be right along; I just need to load my mule." Beth joyfully expressed.

"Excuse me your highness, I believe some of this equipment is expressly yours?"

"Oh, how silly of me, of course!" As she reached for a small bag and attempted to walk away.

David reached out quickly and grabbed her arm, pulling her back a bit, "A little professionalism, if you please?"

"Sorry, I am trying to add some comedy to hide the fear." He let go.

"I understand, but we could really use a positive evaluation, no one will come to us for help if everyone thinks we are jackasses and incompetent. Save the levity till we are alone." They both turned and look toward Mary, who stood there, having watched the whole show.

They can see in her face she was questioning this choice already.

"Come on you two, daylight is burning and I do not want to be here past sundown ...no offense."

"It's okay, we understand and we are ready." Beth calmly added.

After about an hour hike, they reached the area where the remains were discovered. There was still police tape wrapped around the trees, cordoning off a rectangular area. Immediately David broke out his electronic gear, lights, cameras, thermal sensors, etc. Beth started to walk the perimeter around the tape, she was focused and getting in tune with the energies around her. Something dark and malevolent, a hunger ...a hunger that never stops......never.... She pulled herself back, a cold shiver ran down her whole body.

"I think we are right on the money with our evaluation." At this point David carefully walked through the taped off area.

He studied the ground and took pictures and video footage.

"Whatever it was, it was exceptionally large and walked on two legs. Given the size, I would have figured a deeper impression in the ground, but then again, what we are dealing with."

"Yes, it's tall but still very thin and gaunt." Beth added.

"What exactly are you two talking about, what kind of animal do you think it is?" Mary asked.

"Look, I know you asked us to investigate, but I am not sure you are ready to hear what we think. Maybe it's just better to let us handle this, we will call when it's over." Said David.

"Look, I don't need to be handled or patronized, I just wanna know what happened to my friend."

Beth stepped forward, "it's called a Wendigo, its less an animal and more a curse, more than likely some backwoodsman or lost camper did something awful out here and was struck down."

"Struck down, what do you mean?" Mary said with an air of confusion.

"If a person resorts to let us say...cannibalism, the spirits of the woods may inflict upon them a curse, for violating natural law and betraying their companions. The Wendigo is strong, fast and is an excellent hunter. Its hunger never wains, they will however hibernate from time to time, but so long as it's awake, it's hungry." Mary looked shocked; she couldn't believe what she was hearing.

"This is what you think is out here, what you think killed my friend? So, if this is true, how are you going to deal with it?"

David stepped back into the conversation, "Well, it is not exactly alive, more like a force, but a good blast of silver will put it down for a while. Then we salt and burn the remains and then the coup de gras, a counter curse ending the threat permanently.

Otherwise, it could rise again at some point."

Beth added, "Of course if some nitwit repeats the act, it could start all over again." Mary was still confused and bewildered. She was struggling to understand any of this, being a Wildlife Biologist, this whole thing is completely counterintuitive to her thoughts. This story defied logic and science. She thought when she contacted them, they were some kind of new-age investigators, maybe have a new slant on being a detective and discover something the cops missed, something that proved it was murder and not an animal attack. Or perhaps some kind of cryptozoologist group and would find evidence of some new species to explain this situation. Something concrete and still valid. Finding out they think it's some kind of magical curse in the form of a monster was not what she expected, at all. David could see she was still lost and maybe regretted calling them.

"Look, I get it, it's a lot to take in and it seems crazy as hell, but just let us do our thing and if it doesn't work, we will try something else or get lost, whatever you want." Mary just eyed them up and down and then nodded.

Mary didn't say anything else, she simply started back down the path back to her truck. The two looked at each other with resolve.

Doing his best to track its movements, David found a clearing further into the woods from the attack. The Hunter laid snare traps with silver/magnesium flares. The traps are not meant to trap it, but rather distract and surprise the creature and set it up for a clean shot. Unfortunately, there is no high point to sit at, for a clean shot. The Witch was able to perch herself on a good cross-section of tree limbs, but she doesn't need the same kind of vantage point, her awareness doesn't need line of site to work.

Hours had gone by, Dave had spread his own blood over a large radius, trailing it back to their little clearing from a few specific directions. He sat, shotgun in hand, just quietly contemplating his tiny campfire and various scenarios, not knowing what way it will approach. Suddenly

Beth sat up in her perch, "something is near, get ready."

"Any idea on a direction ...it would be helpful"

"I am working on it, this isn't GPS I got here, yah know!"

"I know...just trying not to panic or pee!"

"With your diet, that might actually make it back off!"

"Nice, preservative jokes! What next, fat jokes?"

"Just trying to keep things light, before you die, horribly." Beth muses.

"You mean, before we, don't you?"

"Um... no, I am in the tree, I never read a single thing about them climbing, besides I can run while it fills up on your cheeseburger/chili/pizza ass."

Before David could send another zinger her way, a loud snap of wood echoed from beyond the clearing.

"I got the direction now, what are you sensing?"

"It's strange, I can't seem to pinpoint it, it seems to be in two places ...either this thing is way faster than we thought or.... Oh shit, get out of there!"

Just then a flare fires off from directly in front of him, he raised the shotgun only to be distracted by another flare going off, directly behind him as Beth screamed to him. "There are two!" His eyes widened; his pupils dilated to the point of making his eyes look all black! Ahead of him a creature stepped into the light of his campfire. It was gaunt and putrid looking, its head was a rotted deer, with a huge disfigured maw, gaping with huge, tusk-like teeth! David did not move, even as he felt the approach of the second, as the Witch continued to scream for him to move.

At that moment, she reached for a pouch, she lit it up with a match and hurled it at the one behind David. It hit in front of the smaller creature and made a small pop that released a cloud of silver and other ingredients into the air! The creature withdrew and choked from the exposure. In this same moment the larger beast, some 13 feet in height, charged with its head forward, mouth open and dripping with saliva, antlers aimed for David. Before it reached him, a large blast rang out and the creature stumbled but still caught David with an antler tip. David figured the top of its head, with its thick bone and antlers may be a little too tough, so he aimed for the knee with the best shot line. As he hit his mark, he tried to turn towards the smaller, choking beast, maybe 9 feet in height. Even though the larger one's antler struck home, David still fired off another shot toward the smaller one. The creature recoiled as it screamed a horrible cry. David pumped the weapon and fired again in the blink of an eye, right at the same spot. The creature dropped to its knees and slumped forward, face into the ground. At that moment the larger one had risen and restarted its charge, David dove to his left and rolled, racking another round. As he rolled up, he now looked it right in the face! The beast opened wide and sunk two of its tusk-like front teeth, into David's shoulder when a familiar pop rang out and silver filled the air around them.

The beast inhaled and immediately choked, releasing its bite. The hunter rolled again, out from under it and fired without hesitation. The blast struck its back but did not kill it. The blow did spin it towards him, racking another round he leveled a heart shot. It made a similar scream but was not dead yet. He racked and pulled the trigger only to hear an unfortunate click. He dove into his coat pocket as the beast began to recover, loaded, racked and fired! Still the creature was not done. He scrambled for his last shell, got to his feet, as the creature rose its head. David lunged and rammed the barrel down its throat and pulled the trigger. The beast dropped.

"Well, that was unexpected and quite horrible." Beth proclaimed.

"I agree, there was not a damn thing that suggested there was another, what the hell? All I can figure is someone else turned while this first was hunting. It was smaller and so had not fed on as much as the first." David said in an exhausted tone. "Thank the powers that you laid all those flare traps." Beth replied. "And thank you Beth, for having made those silver grenades. They gave me the time I needed to finish them off. Okay, come on down and get started on the counter curse components, while I salt and burn the shit out of these things." David added.

Beth came down from the tree and got a better look at David's wounds. A puncture in his side and two bite marks in his left shoulder. The wounds had sealed up slightly, so there was little blood, so long as he did not move much.

"We need to get you to a hospital; this is not good at all." Beth sounded nervous.

"Its but a scratch!" David retorted.

"Could you be serious for a minute? You could have died...right there, right in front of me and I would not have been able to do anything!" Beth was loud and fear permeated her tone.

David's look changed, "Hey, it's done, we survived and we have saved people. Not to mention we will be ending their pain, those two trapped as monsters."

"I know we did... but." Beth trailed off, not finishing her thought.

"What is it Beth? You have been on edge with each new adventure, am I doing something wrong?" Beth paused, the honesty in his question shook her out of her worry.

"No, you were awesome, absolutely awesome, I am just tired."

"Well, let's get this business finished and get back to the hotel to rest."

After the fires burned out, Beth finished her spell work on

both of them. She then consecrated the ground and David buried what was left of them. They returned to the hotel, just in time for breakfast to start. They got to their room for a quick clean up and then back down for more bacon. During breakfast David called Mary to report that the creature had been handled. The killings should be over for now. She thanked them a lot, but still had a confused and non-believing tone when she asked for details. The *thank-you* had a genuine sound though.

David turned to Beth after calling Mary. "Well, we still have a couple days, no reason to rush, I wasn't sure how long it would take, so I made it a really long weekend."

Beth turned to him and said, "I appreciate that, but I really need to get home, do you still have those tickets?"

"I am sorry, I changed them out."

"Oh okay, well ...wait you changed them out for what?"

"An open-ended ticket to come to Hibbing, Minnesota. I called Brianne, she flies in tomorrow, so we need to drive down in the morning and pick her up."

"What the, how the......Oh wow ...When did you do all this?"

"After we got back to the hotel, while you were cleaning up. The ticket, I changed the other day...also while you were cleaning up ...I had more time that morning! After breakfast I will also set up another room for myself, so you two can have some privacy."

Beth was beaming, "You sir, are amazing."

"I know, all the ladies say so!" David said with a stupid grin.

Darren Anderson

Beth Didn't even care about the stupid joke, she only cares that he is a true friend and that she can rest in the arms of her lover on the next day.

CHAPTER FIVE

As their day started, Beth was comfortably snuggled into her wife. Beth, instead of sleeping, was listening to her breath, or more specifically snore! With each noisy exhale her smile broadened and her mind began to drift towards the past. She started to reflect upon her life and on the road that led to where she is now.

She remembered her youth and the time she spent in the woods listening to the trees and the life that flowed through the land. It relaxed her, allowed her to shut out the chaos of modern life. The more time she spent among the wild, natural things of the world, the stronger her connection became.

She was often mocked in school and other social situations. She was the freak, the outcast, the loser. Kids have always been cruel to what they could not understand. It took her a long time to realize that other people did not have a natural connection to the world around them. They lived on the world, not in it and they could not begin to fathom or even believe her connection. When she spoke about the trees imparting wisdom and the foxes spreading humor, the other children thought she was crazy, or just a liar. As she moved through higher grades in school her interactions with other children waned strongly. Even the kids who purported to be children of nature were clueless to the truth of existence. Yah, they were posers. Beth remembered. Sweet, but they had no idea what being a Witch truly was. Their knowledge came from cheesy movies and a few select history books.

As her connection to everything grew, so did the disparity with other people, even her own family. They, like the kids in school, had no understanding of the natural world or her grasp of it. So instead of withdrawing from her connection, she decided to broaden her knowledge base. She consumed any piece of information she could find. The age of technology and the world of the internet ironically helped her initially achieve a new understanding of the natural world and what she was turning into. This new discovery led to her finding other people who were more in line with her understandings. Granted she had to pour through a whole slew of people who were also clueless, or flower children who never made it out of the '60s. Eventually she found genuine articles, people who knew the wisdom of the trees. It was in the first meeting with Angela Ashcroft that she received her first real education. Angela recognized her immediately as a kindred person. When Beth walked into her little apothecary, Angela perked up, looked at her as though she was looking into her soul and then smiled.

"Oh my dear, you will do!" She enthusiastically reported.

Beth's eyes broadened wider than her smile. She had no idea she had just enrolled in Witchcraft 101.

For the next few years she would spend as much time as she could visiting Angela's shop and learning from Angela and her sisters. She was welcomed into their group with open minds and hearts. She learned the importance of various herbs, roots, and oils. Beth learned all about the celestial movements, the true nature of Fae Folk and eventually about the darker things that exist in the world.

Potions and spells along with their components were memorized and cataloged. Ways that the simplest things could help and heal anything from physical ailments to emotional distress. She began to wonder if there was more to this new life, then learning and making special concoctions? She addressed the group, specifically Angela, about what is wrong with the world and the darker things that plague it and its peoples.

The entire history of what goes bump in the night, what stalks humankind and what things lie beyond the veil was unfolded before her. Sometimes knowledge can be harmful, sometimes not knowing allows one to live a better life. Beth wished she did not know this side of things. She wished she could go back to just being a child of nature and enjoy her connections to life. The importance of helping displaced or trapped spirits, cursed people and confused entities was explained. The group tried their hardest to impress upon her that not everything beyond the veil or moving in the shadows were completely evil. Many times, they were misunderstood, trapped and wronged in a way that they cannot escape from or undo on their own. That is part of the responsibility of those who walk in this world, who live within it, instead of just on it.

The thought of fighting or even helping these beings ran a shudder through her core. Beth felt overwhelmed and terrified. The group tried to console her and get her to relax, but it was no use. Beth withdrew, all she had wanted was a place to be understood, a place to be accepted. She was not looking to be a warrior for the world or savior for lost spirits. It was too much, too soon. Beth had graduated high school, so she relocated. She could not go home again, it was too much to try and refit back into that lifestyle, to pretend to be something else again. She then decided upon a new place, someplace where she could be herself, be free, but not have to bear the weight of the world upon her shoulders or engage in spiritual warfare.

A sudden loud snort shattered her remembrance. The groggy, disapproving eye of Brianne slowly focused upon her face. The first image that became clear was the smiling eyes of Beth.

"Ugh, how long have you been laying there, staring at me?" She softly growled.

"Not long, I was enjoying the melody being created."

"Coffee ...need coffee...no talking ...coffee." The Wolf sluggishly rose from their bed and stumbled for the kitchen where a pot was already brewed.

"Oh, I love you." The Wolf called out.

"I know." She enjoyed making fandom references, especially when they fit perfectly into conversations.

Beth began to bunch up the blankets and wrap them around herself. She began to drift back into her memories. Over the months that followed, after she departed the group, she had settled into a new life. She had moved a couple towns away from her family and the group. She did not want to accidentally bump into anyone. She wanted a fresh start. She worked in a sales department for a major department store chain. It was not glamorous, but it paid the bills and she was making friends. As a matter of fact, she made a very good friend. That was Alicia, they worked together. Alicia was bubbly, upbeat and always smiling. Alicia was born in Georgia, but her family moved while she was fairly young for work. She still had a hint of a Georgian accent when certain words escaped her lips. She tended to call people sweetie and the southern twang could be heard loud and clear. Alicia was slight of frame, with crystal blue eyes and dirty blond hair which she changed when the mood suited her. She was a true southern belle in appearance and attitude. They started with lunchtime meetups. Then came the occasional dinner, then games of pool at the bar. Movies were worked in sometimes.

Then eventually they were together for breakfast, but not because they met up. Beth enjoyed their relationship. It was fun and flirty. It was consistent and most importantly to Beth, it was normal. No craft, to spirits, just life. Beth rejoiced in their mediocrity.

One day while staying at the Witch's place, Alicia stumbled onto some of her notes, a basic book of instructions for various spells and concoctions. What in the world is this? Alicia thought to herself. Beth was cleaning up, after both had woken up. They were planning a little picnic later for their shared day off. Alicia was thumbing through the book with ravenous curiosity. Flipping through page after page, she was trying to absorb as much as she could. She had completely lost track of time and awareness of her surroundings. So, it was no surprise that she had not noticed Beth walk back into the room and park herself right next to Alicia.

"Find anything interesting?" Beth said with a smile.

"Oh yes, this is some really wild stuff?" Alicia's eyes never left the pages.

Realizing Beth was next to her, her eyes slowly rose from the book and turned towards Beth.

"Oh sweetie, I am so sorry, I didn't mean to be nosy...I."

"You didn't huh? Lotta reading for someone to accidentally accomplish." Her tone was dripping with sarcasm and her smile was broad and warm.

"Don't tease," she lilted, "I didn't mean to dig, but it was right here and...and...I need a lifeline sweetie." Alicia was trying to be cute, but her embarrassment was shining through.

"It's okay, you wanna know something, ask."

Okay, so first ...are you a witch or something? Like Marie Laveau?"

Beth laughed out loud! "Well...the simple short answer is yes, but it goes a little deeper than that, but I am not practicing as much as I did anymore."

Her face seemed to lose a little joy for a moment, "How come you don't practice as much ...did the villagers chase you with torches?"

"First of all, that has to do with the movie Frankenstein, not about Witchcraft. Second, you are a smart-ass. So, what else is on your mind?"

Alicia practically screamed out, "Can we do a spell? Contact a spirit, change something into something else?"

"Whoa, settle down, I am not a stage magician. There is a lot more involved than just waving my hand and throwing out some weird made-up words." Beth had taken a more serious tone; her expression had become harder.

"Sorry, I didn't mean to offend or make fun, I just got really excited. I mean this isn't real or anything right, it's just fun or a peaceful philosophy, right?"

Beth stood there for a moment, perplexed as to what to say, how to answer her.

"Look, it's easier if I show you."

Alicia now looked puzzled, "Show me what, sweetie?"

Darren Anderson

Beth ignored her for a moment. She pulled a mirror and some candles along with a small vial of oil. She placed the candles in a order along with the mirror. She poured the oil into a small bowl along with some herbs. Under her breath she began to mutter some words. Alicia could not make them out, but it did not sound like English. Beth kept repeating them as she lit the candles and assumed a particular body position. Alicia was starting to feel silly, in fact she was holding back a giggle when suddenly, an aura began to envelop the Witch. The energy seemed to be emanating from the mirror across from her. Beth's face seemed to change, small imperfections were melting away, her hair went from looking half-dried to perfectly styled. Her face also seemed to look like she had her makeup done already. Alicia's face told the whole story. Her mouth was gaping, her eyes were wide and bright. She thought this was a game, that it was not real. She was very wrong. Beth stopped the incantation and blew out the candles and started to put everything away. Alicia was still sitting there, staring at the spot where the Witch had been sitting.

"Alicia, are you with me?"

"I...uh ...um, yah, I am here. So, this stuff, this is real?"

"Yup, very real. I don't even know what to say, but I creeped you out a bit, huh?" Beth said, feeling a little nervous.

"No...I mean, well yeah, a little, but no that was awesome! I wanna know more!"

"Easy, there tiger, I am not a teacher and this is not the kind of stuff you play with if you don't know what you are doing.

Shadow Walking

There are doors that can be opened that are very hard to close. So, you gotta promise me, not to do things without me, this isn't playtime stuff." Alicia promised.

Beth felt odd, she had closed off this part of her life and in the blink of an eye she was right back into old habits. She had walked away for a reason and she should probably stick to that thought.

Beth shifted on her bed. The memories started to unsettle her. Their time had passed and was wonderful, but a moment would come and redirect her life permanently. The echo of the warning Beth gave Alicia had completely faded. Alicia's curiosity for this new world only continued to grow and engulf her entire life. Suddenly there was scarcely time for anything else in her life. She wanted to learn and expand her skills. Beth thought it was cute at first, then endearing. Later though, it began to worry her. It was a once in a while moment to share a spell or learn a piece of history. Now, it's all Alicia wanted to do or talk about. New mixtures, new spells, and new concepts. It reminded herself of back when she first discovered her coven, all the excitement and new discoveries. However, the final revelation, the cost of this knowledge, was more than she was willing to pay. This means she had hit the limit of what she could teach Alicia. The dangers were ambiguous at best. Beth did not stay long enough to learn the specifics, to learn about the real dangers. If she knew, she could have stressed the warnings stronger, made the dangers more real in her mind. Perhaps Alicia would have backed off her desires.

Darren Anderson

Alicia wanted to surprise her, to show her how much she had learned. It was Beth's birthday and she wanted to call forth an image, a colorful fox, something she would find adorable. A perfect "I love you." It would have been better if she had waited and got some help. Beth arrived home, called out to Alicia, but there was no answer. She must be shopping or something, I wonder if I need to start dinner? She moved through the apartment, placing her work bag down, sifted through the mail and moved towards the bedroom to change and get comfortable. As she moved into the bedroom, she noticed all kinds of items placed around the room. Special items, summoning items, something went down. What the hell did she do? As she rounded the bed, she found her, slumped over onto the floor. Immediately she rushed to her side, she lifted her up and checked for a pulse and her breathing. As Beth touched her, she noticed how cold she was. Alicia had passed, no markings, no wounds. Jesus Christ Alicia, what did you do? Her eyes passed over the items, then moved to the pages that were open. As she read, she realized what she may have been after. Some form of summoning spell. She was probably trying to conjure something cute, something adorable, but I think you misinterpreted a step. After reading more of the pages and rechecking the items, it was clear that when she opened the door, something pulled her through, astrally.

Alicia probably didn't even know she was walking without her body. Passing through the threshold, she must have trapped herself or got herself lost. Beth immediately gathered everything for a summoning spell, she had to call her back before her body was beyond saving. Beth tried, she called out, she reached out with everything she had, used every essence of her being. A voice called back to her. "It's too late child, she is beyond your reach."

"Who are you? How do you know, do you have her, let her go!" Beth was panicked and desperate.

"I am a friend, I did not take her, but she is gone." Please. Please, help me! I need to bring her back, it's my fault, I can't just leave her!"

"She made a choice child, just as you did. I am sorry." Beth pleaded and demanded help, but the voice was silent.

Beth struggled to find a trace of Alicia, but it was no use, Alicia was gone. Beth broke down and cried for a long time and cursed her lack of experience. Beth cursed her choice to quit, to walk away. If she stayed with it, this never would have happened. Even if it had still happened, she would have known how to save Alicia.

Back in the bed, Beth wiped her eyes. A small trail of tears stained her face and moistened her pillow. She never found Alicia beyond the veil. By the time she stopped searching, it was too late, Alicia's body was beyond inhabiting. She had to call the ambulance and report the incident. The Medical Examiner was at a loss. No sign of drugs, no sign of violence or poison. It was a mystery, just one of those freak moments. This was no relief to Alicia's family and friends. While the doctors could offer no cause for her death, the family knew all they needed to. The lifestyle, her weird ways, her ungodly life. After that, no one around Beth trusted her. Always there was a look of disdain in their eyes. The family would not even speak to her except to explain that she was not welcome at the funeral. After the service, when everyone had left, she visited the grave. Beth knelt, wept, and apologized for not being there, for not teaching her better, for not being able to save her.

This was a turning point in her life. One where she finally decided to embrace what she truly was, a guardian of this world. Beth moved back home and reconnected with her group. She apologized for her fear and lack of understanding. She explained about Alicia and what had happened. Together they mourned the passing but rejoiced in having Beth back on her path. Since then she has become a stronger person, not just in her knowledge, but to her dedication to helping all life.

The tears had stopped flowing and contentment filled her face. She could hear her wife starting her work, several zaps, zots, twangs and all manner of other gaming sounds were calling out from the living room. She grabbed a mug of coffee and stood against the wall, watching her wife frantically attempting to resolve a game glitch. The fountain of profanity spewing from her mouth was almost musical to her as she fully embraced her place in this world.

CHAPTER SIX

David was lying in bed, fast asleep when his cell phone fired off a loud and disturbing Godzilla Roar! He rolled over and scrambled to get to it, if only to silence the noise. Groggily he answered the phone, not bothering to check the number or Id.

"Hello?" The familiar soft tone of Beth filled his ear.

"Well, good morning Sunshine, how are you?"

"Ughh, sigh…what do you want?" David groaned.

"Just wanted to remind you I will be out of town for a bit. I have a Witchcraft Convention to attend."

"Wait, that sounds sorta tacky and superficial, considering what you have actually done in your life, doesn't that annoy you?"

"Well, yes, a little bit, but they have great deals on ingredients and items. They sell totems and medallions that they have no idea about or how valuable and powerful they are!! It's like when you go to a flea market and find a first edition comic for a quarter, I almost feel bad for the people selling things!"

David smiled into the phone, "But you buy the stuff anyway and never tell, do you?"

"Oh, hell no, I need those things! So anyway, I wanted you to know, in case you had something lined up, I won't be around for a few days."

"Okay mom, I will be fine without you, go fleece your wannabe, hipster, witches." Beth ignored that comment. "Just be careful, you have a tendency to get in over your head and I won't be around to save your a..."

"Goodbye..." And just like that David hung up.

Later, after David cleaned himself up and cooked up some eggs and bacon, he headed down to the office to check the feed for any unusual events or stories. As he was sifting through thousands of stories, news reports and whack job firsthand accounts. He came across something interesting in Denver, Colorado. Six people have been found dead. Two of them were children, 8 and 10 years old. Another two were each child's mother and the last two were an elderly couple. Not exactly riveting news at first glance, Denver is a fairly large city, murder is a downside. So, David looked deeper into the article in case there were some other factors to make it relevant. Nothing was standing out, except that each of the attacks took place outside of a Catholic Church, a Mosque and a Jewish Temple. Each holy place was within a few blocks of each other. David was wondering, was it just a hate crime situation or was there an angry demon, some old God not impressed with modern worship. I need to look a little deeper into this. David whispered to himself. Guess it's time to break out my journalistic credentials! I mean the courts did rule that having a blog equated to journalism.

David spent the rest of the day stocking the van with reference books, various defensive charms, inscriptions and potions that Beth had left him in case of an emergency and he also brought his EMP-Ghost Gun. On top of that, David also made sure to load his shotgun with his 'kitchen sink' ammo. Inspired by some pop culture and movies, David created shotgun rounds loaded with white oak shavings, silver, salt, clove, iron filings and blessed water. It was guaranteed to take out almost anything. David also made sure to grab his "INS Reporter" credentials. David had started a blog a few years back. It was mostly about mythological and supernatural happenings, but he still investigated and reported on stories around the country, so in his mind that made him a genuine journalist. In his mind he hoped the cops would see it that way as well. After all, it's hard to do a proper investigation without checking the crime scenes. David felt excited and slightly apprehensive. Ever since he met Beth, real monsters, spirits and demons have poured out of the woodwork. In the beginning, he was lucky to get a beep on an

EMF Meter, now full torso apparitions manifested and tore rooms apart, extra-dimensional creatures attempted to possess him and he has even had to hunt down not one, but two Wendigos. Life has taken a turn he never expected. David had always believed or at least wanted to believe in supernatural phenomena, but he had never really found anything noteworthy till Beth came into his life. Now he feels a little worried not having her by his side. Partly because he has no real clue yet, what he is heading towards. The unknown can be a little creepy, but also very exciting!

The next morning David rose, had breakfast, double-checked his equipment list and made sure he had his phone and charger. He was going to wait until he hit Denver to find a small-time hotel to crash at, one that he could extend his stay as he needed to. David then hopped into his van and headed to Denver. Tuning his police scanner to the proper frequency, David caught the call for a 10-54, possible fatality. It would seem another dead body had been discovered around the very same Catholic Church that the Mother and her son were found the previous week.

David activated his GPS, time to let the technology do the navigating to get him to the church on time. David pulled off onto a side street and grabbed his phone, a notepad, pen and a small digital camera, along with his INS ID Card. David approached the crime scene slowly, not because he was nervous, but because he wanted to get the lay of the land and make sure he didn't miss any obvious clues that this may be just a basic homicide. The officers had cordoned off an area around behind the church, near the mouth of an alley. David approached and was immediately stopped by an officer.

"Can I help you, sir?"

David struggled for his makeshift press ID, "Um, sorry, yes, I am the Press, I am with INS News, Internet News Site."

The cop looked at the credentials and then looked back at David with a disapproving stare.

"This doesn't look like a standard press pass."

"Oh, I'm from out of town, we go all over, ya know, internet news." David said with a sheepish look.

"Okay, just don't disturb anything and stay out of forensics way."

"Not a problem Officer!"

The Medical Examiner was removing the body, David ran over quick to sneak a look. The body had been mostly devoured.

"So, Doc, is there a cause of death?"

"It's going to require some further examination, there is too much tissue damage at this time to be able to determine anything, now if you can excuse me." The body was loaded and David turned his attention back to the officer.

"Excuse me, do you think this was a mugging gone wrong or what?"

"Well first of all, no. His wallet, ID's, cash, everything was still there. That is how we were able to get an identification already."

"Ahh, so the victim's name? Robert Wilson, age 34. And

Robert was killed last night? Lotta tissue loss for less than 24 hours?"

"Obviously the report is off. The rats must have been at this body for longer than expected. The witness must have heard something else and stumbled onto the body, a simple coincidence of situations."

David perked up, "There was a witness?"

"Like I said, a person found the body and claimed to have heard a guy scream beforehand. Obviously, the person heard something else and then found a body that has been here for a few days and every muncher has had their part."

"Can I get the name of the witness?"

"Yes, it's Mr. Lou Scheiber, he found the body and claimed to have heard the scream."

"Well, thank you for your time, Officer." Before David departed, he took several crime scene photos.

Pictures of where the body was found and the areas all around, in case there were prints, signs or markings, anything that could tell him what this was.

David found a cheap motel and moved in. He set up his computer and began to dig further throughout the local news websites about what was happening in the city. Over the last six months, there had been eighteen incidents, all revolving around the same areas as the church, mosque and temple. All the bodies had apparently suffered major tissue damage, as though several creatures had fed upon them. Strangely enough, way back at the beginning when the first victim was found the former lead medical examiner gave a different explanation. He had said, on the record, that all the wounds were created by the same set of teeth and that whatever it was, was much larger than any rat, cat or dog in the area. Also, whatever it was, fed no more than 24 hours before the body had been discovered. Dr. Westmoore, just a couple months later, retired. He retired just after he recanted his earlier explanation.

He stated that he must have misread the information and that the body must have gone undiscovered for a much longer period of time. Well, that isn't suspicious at all, is it? Scheiber swears he heard a scream and then discovered the body. So, if he is correct, whatever it is, killed Wilson, consumed a healthy portion of him and got out of there before Scheiber could get there.

Vampires don't usually eat any flesh and not that much, Werewolves will chow down, but the bites are obvious and again, the quantity is too high. Weights and Ghouls prefer older meat, they kill then they stow the meat, preferring a bit of rot. A Wendigo could eat that much or more, but they are a bit more obvious in their methods and not usually a city dweller...plus a 12 or so foot tall monster with a rotted stag head kinda stands out. So, what in the fiery frack am I dealing with, if I am dealing with something. *More research it is!* I must be missing something, maybe I got something in my pics, that I didn't see initially. David took out his digital camera and scrolled through the pics. Two things stood out after he poured over the pics. First, there was a tremendous amount of debris and trash near the body, but no trash cans, dumpsters or any other receptacles. The other thing that stood out was in the pictures of the church, along one of its sides. There seemed to be feces and other materials smeared upon the side of the church. At first glance it just seemed nasty and random, but as David looked, he realized the smears seemed to form specific patterns and shapes, almost a written language. After a couple hours of pouring through the internet for matching symbols, David finally discovered that it was in fact writing and was closest to Hindi. Comparing as best as he could, he determined that the crap writing was essentially nothing more than taunts. 'God is a lie, prayer yields empty'? Okay, a translator I am not, however I think I have the gist of the sentiment. Something hates the church; I wonder if there are similar script at the other sites? So, a supernatural hate crime? Am I dealing with a racist demon or something? David called it quits for the night and went to sleep.

In the morning David went to the other sites, the Temple and the Mosque. While walking around both buildings, he discovered remnants of what could have been writing. The members of each group must have cleaned up after the crimes as best as they could without disturbing the crime scene. As he walked around, David noticed another building, a temple of sorts, but not a Mosque or Jewish Temple. He walked a few blocks and came to a Hindu Temple. David checked the address and compared it to the information for all the recent murders.

Shadow Walking

None of the bodies were discovered at this site, yet it is not far from the Catholic Church, or the other sites for that matter. David walked around the building looking for similar signs, trash, feces smeared, weird lettering. None of that was discovered, however there were symbols painted at each corner and along the sides. One was similar to a Nazi Swastika. David remembered that the Nazis stole the symbol from the Hindu religion and altered it a bit to make their symbol. For the Hindu faith, the symbol represents peace and protection amongst other things. The other symbol he was not familiar with, but he had a way to find out. David went into the temple, looking for a priest. The search did not take long. David walked to the gentleman, dressed in a three-quarter length red coat, covered in ornate writing. He also had a garment hanging from his neck which looked like a yellow scarf.

"Namaste, how may I help you."

"Hello, my name is David and I was looking for a priest or religious representative, I had some odd questions."

"Well I am the Pujari here, the Priest as you would say, my name is Abhi Khatri, what sort of questions do you have?"

The man spoke perfect English, with a hint of a Hindi accent.

"This may come off as rude, so let me apologize in advance, but I was curious about Hindu demons or monsters."

"You seem to be asking in earnest, I take no offense, what specifically did you want to know?"

"Offhand, is there something in your history that would consume nearly an entire person in a short span of time, really shredding the body and would look to desecrate a holy site? Such as leaving slurs and anti-religious rhetoric."

"Well, that is somewhat of an odd question, however I am quite sure I know what you are asking about. The beast you seem to be describing is a servant of Ravana, a Rakshasa."

"A Rak..sha..ssa?"

"Yes, a particularly loathsome and cowardly creature, it has a nearly insatiable hunger for human flesh and can easily strip a person down to bones in a small matter of time. They are horrible to behold, red slitted eyes, shaggy, red, coarse hair and large tusks as well as claws. Of course, the worst thing to keep in mind is that the Rakshasa has the ability to use magic and illusions ...they will creep into your mind and assume a form you trust to trick you into allowing them to get close enough to slaughter you."

David's eyes had grown larger as the man spoke, "Well, that sounds completely horrible, so they also send hate letters?"

"Oh yes, the Rakshasa will look to disrupt any prayer or religious assemblies, they detest them, they also feed upon refuse and delight in throwing it at temples and similar structures." David's brow now furled.

"That explains the writing on the walls and all the trash, without any dumpsters around. These places that have been tormented, they are not far from here, yet I see no signs of disruption around your temple at all."

"I am a servant of Brahma and Vishnu, it is my duty to repel such loathsome creatures, so I have painted the Swastika and the Om all over the area. These symbols protect this temple and repel the Rakshasa, the filthy beast would never come near this place."

David looked a little happier, knowing the symbols that could repel them.

"You have been unbelievably helpful, but now the big question, how do you kill or otherwise get rid of a Rakshasa?"

"A brass dagger or brass tipped arrow or bolt piercing the heart will destroy a Rakshasa permanently. If you are intent on hunting one, I have a dagger you may have. It is blessed by Brahma, but you must be careful, the beast will know you as well as you know yourself. It will find an image to trick you, to lull you into dropping your guard and if you do, you will die as if being ripped apart by several wild animals all at once."

"I appreciate your concern and warnings, but this creature, if that is what it is, must be put down."

"I understand and I admire your courage for wanting to face this beast, let me get the dagger." David took the dagger and thanked the Pujari a few more times.

He then asked one final question, "So, how can I draw this creature out?"

"Ahh yes, go to the areas where he has been feeding after nightfall, he is weak in the day and will not hunt until the sun is down. Begin a personal prayer or chant, whatever means the most to you, the Rakshasa will be drawn to your prayer and seek to end it and you. Please, please be careful, it will find a way to trick you."

David made his way to a sporting goods store. He decided to increase his odds and purchased some brass pellets, so he could load them into his shotgun shells. David also stopped by a craft store and picked up some small, wooden square blocks. Things he could easily carry and carve some protection symbols into. After his trip to the sporting goods and craft stores, David returned to his hotel room to change out a dozen shells, do a little carving and to bring up a map of the area. He needed to find a place that he could lure the Rakshasa into while limiting the directions it could approach. David didn't need it creeping up behind him like the second Wendigo did. David found a tight alley near the Jewish Temple and decided to wait. After a couple hours he remembered the part about prayer drawing one in and decided now was a good time to start his.

David wasn't sure what to do. Recite a Catholic prayer, acknowledge one of Beth's spirits, Brahma, Buddha, something else? Finally, he just decided to just sort of have a conversation with God.

"Well, God, here I am, hunting another of your questionable creations before someone else ends up as Alpo. I was raised Catholic, but I could never really get on board with it...I suppose it's my ass if I made the wrong choice...on the upside, I will have some great company!"

So, I... Just then a bottle went tumbling, as though someone or something had kicked it aside. David raised a flashlight and began to draw his sawed-off pump shotgun from his backpack when another familiar sound came from behind him. The sound of a police car chirp. David quickly let the shotgun drop back into his pack and dropped his hand and turned around.

"What exactly are you doing here?" The officer, who was now out of his car, asked.

"Hello there, Officer! I am a reporter with INS Internet News Service. I was doing some follow up leg work on the recent homicides in this area." The Officer did not look impressed.

"Given the recent issues with wild animals, I can't advise you to hang around too long in this area, Sir. I think maybe you should wrap it up and go home."

"Uh, okay Officer." David took the hint, nothing was gonna happen tonight, leastways, nothing involving the Supernatural.

David got back to the hotel room, dropped his backpack and laid on the bed to watch some television. He looked to his side and realized he had left his phone in the room the whole day. He picked it up and noticed he had a missed call from Beth. Apparently earlier today she had found some time in her busy schedule of screwing local yokels out of valuable Wiccan materials to check in on him. "Aww, Mom misses me! She didn't leave a message though, so she doesn't miss me that much." David decided it was a little late and that maybe he should call her tomorrow. He thought about the sounds he heard, before the cops spoiled the trap. I think tomorrow night, I will hide at the other end of the alley. If the cops find me again in the same place,

I think they might run me in for questioning. I don't really need to explain how I am there to hunt a Rakshasa and of course I need a shotgun and a brass knife and a couple warding symbols. Yah, that will be a great trip to court.

The next day David cleaned up and went for breakfast. Before leaving, he stopped by the Front Desk to extend his stay for another night. David approached the barely aware clerk.

"Good morning."

The clerk only replied with, "Checking Out?"

"Actually...no, I was wondering if I could keep the same room for another night at least?" The clerk looked confused and blankly stared for a couple seconds.

After the wheels started rolling again, he punched some information into his small desktop computer and said, "Okay, you are set for another night, enjoy your stay."

The sentiment was made with the lowest amount of enthusiasm possible and still be breathing. David tried to call Beth at breakfast, but couldn't get through, cell phone dead zone. He decided to scope out the new area he wanted to hide out in, while the sun was up and while he would not have to worry about an unexpected encounter, with either the police or the Rakshasa. The area looked about as good as can be expected. It looked inviting, rather pleasant. Amazing what a lack of sunlight can do for the ambiance of an area. How forbidding and creepy it can be, just because it was dark. Well, because of the dark and because there is some Hindu demon lurking, waiting to feast.,

David thought to himself.

Returning to his hotel room, David turned the television on again and zoned out in front of some cooking competition. He was working through the night's activities in his head when he turned to his side just in time to notice his phone shutting off. Apparently, he forgot to charge his phone. He got up and dragged his charger out of his suitcase and plugged it in. I don't have enough on my plate; I need to worry about making sure you are set too? David got back into his bed and continued to plan out the night.

I will lead with the shotgun, see what a few rounds of brass pellets will do to it. If that fails, I will pull the symbols and hope they Bela Legosi it back, while I draw the dagger. If the symbols work like the Pujari said they will, then the Rakshasa should be confused or pained enough to move in for a good strike with the brass dagger.

The day began to wane and David decided he had better get going, he would have to catch up with Guy Fieri another time. David loaded up his pack with the shells and the shotgun, his coat pocket with the dagger and the etched blocks. Just as he walked out the door, he noticed his phone on the charger and ducked back to grab it quick. David decided he would walk to the location, it would give him time to think, plus ensure that the sun would be about down by the time he was in place. I don't wanna have to hang out in the alley, while the sun is up too long. People may get suspicious and ruin my night before it even starts, one more interaction with the police and I might get run out of town or locked up. Neither option worked for me. As he had hoped, by the time he had reached his designated area, the sun had already set and darkness had fallen all around him. Just then a thought popped into his head. Aww Crap! I forgot to call Beth. David reached for his phone and looked it over. I can't worry about it now; I need to keep my head clear. This thing likes to play mind games or, so I have been told, I need to stay clear.

A couple hours past sunset and David decided it was dark enough and time for him to run his spiritual chum line.

"Okay God, I am at again. I am pretty good at what I do, but I could always use a little backup. Yes sir, always can use some help and this is me, asking, rather praying for help." Time seemed to drag a bit.

No sound, no movement as far as he could tell for a while. David wondered if he needed to start his *prayer* again.

"Hey there, God, this is me again, just…" All of a sudden there was rustling down the alleyway.

"Always mumble to yourself like that?" A familiar tone rang out. David drew his shotgun and then his flashlight and shined it down the way. The light fell over a young lady, walking his way. It was Beth.

"Beth, what in the hell are you doing here? Do you know you almost got shot?"

"Easy there, champ, I am not the one who hasn't returned any of my phone calls. Forgive me for being worried." David was happy for a moment, then suspicion drifted in.

"How exactly did you find me, in this town, down this alley?"

"Jeez, paranoid much?"

"Seriously Beth, you need to answer me and answer me now." Beth continued to approach, slowly but steadily.

"It's called GPS genius; I tracked your phone. Not to mention I am a particularly skilled witch; a guiding spell is not out of the question."

"Maybe you are and maybe not, but either way you need to stop, while I think this over."

"I am way too tired and way too done with this, you need to calm down." Beth said in her frustrated tone.

"Seriously Beth, you need to stop, right now!" David demanded.

"Or what, your gonna shoot, leave my wife alone and risk serious jail time for what, cause you think I am some cannibalistic monster?" David's eyes widened.

What kind of monster? David thought to himself.

Realization between the two struck at the speed light. Beth moved like lightning; her striking blow seemed to exceed what her grasp should be at the same time David fired a shot straight at what he thought was her heart. The blow knocked David back into the wall, he winced for a second and when he refocused his eyes, Beth was before him, but something was wrong. Her arm, it was long, muscular, yet gangly and completely covered in reddish/brown coarse hair. Long tusk-like teeth began to protrude from her mouth and her eyes were now blood red. The shot had momentarily stopped her, but it missed its mark. The true location of its heart was not where Beth's would be. All at once a word boomed in David's head, loud, yet not in his ears. The word "Clever" echoed in his mind as the form of Beth began to melt away revealing a horrible sight. Some horrible cross between a human, a rat and a gorilla. The error of his shot became clear and the creature was nearly seven feet tall in its true form. In the moment of revelation, the creature lunged.

David drew one of his etched blocks with the protection symbol from his pocket. The creature unfortunately was fast and knew what was coming. It struck David again both on his hand holding the block and across his chest, knocking him to the other side of the alley. The creature jumped toward David as he lay upon his back, his hand in his coat. The creature landed and immediately a sharp pain filled its mind and a shriek escaped its disgusting lips. David had pushed his dagger through his coat just as it landed. Yet again, the brass had missed its target. The creature was more substantially wounded, but not nearly dead as it rose with the dagger still sticking in it. David immediately drew the other block and cried out 'Brahma protect me.'

The sight of the symbol along with the plea towards Brahma drove the beast back and caused it to cover its eyes. At that moment, David reached out for the dagger and snatched it from the beast's chest. The pain distracted the monster and it lurched toward David. He was finally ready this time and held fast to the etched symbol and again cried out to Brahma as well as Vishnu. Again, the beast recoiled back, this time revealing its chest. Now it was David who lunged forward with all the speed and strength he had and plunged the dagger in once more. Finally, the dagger found its true mark. Just as the beast clenched at David's shoulders, slightly sinking its claws into him. The Rakshasa screamed an unholy cry, one that seemed to shake the very ground they stood upon. As the creature dropped and hit the ground it burst into refuse, guts and dead rats. A disgusting splash of slime coated part of David's face and jacket. The smell was of rotting flesh and putrefied garbage. David hurled a stream of what was left of his dinner. After wrenching, David gathered his gear and started a slow walk back to the hotel, hoping no one would notice him in this state. David reached his room and jumped into the shower to wash off the remnants of his kill. His jacket, however, was a lost cause. He discarded it into the hotel's dumpster. The next day David checked out of the hotel and drove to the Hindu Temple. He wanted to return the brass dagger to Ahbi, the Hindu Pujari.

"I see you were successful in your hunt. I prayed deeply to Brahma that the beast would not take you." David smiled.

"I thank you for that, I needed every bit of help I could get last night. I wanted to give this back to you."

"Oh no, surely Vishnu and Brahma have decided you need this weapon, therefore you should keep it. May the dagger and God's blessings always be in your favor." David did not know what else to say besides thank you.

Upon his drive back home, he wondered what he should tell Beth. Obviously, she is gonna want to know what happened, why didn't he call her back and what did he end up facing. Normally he would jump at the chance to impress her with a good hunting story. This time, however, he must figure out a way to work in the fact that he shot Beth after almost being convinced that it really was her. On the one hand, it shows that Beth is someone he trusts and values and that is why the Rakshasa chose to appear like her. On the other hand, he shot her with a 12 gauge. Well, on the upside, I have a few hours to figure out how to tell this tale in the right way. Just as he was starting to relax from that pleasant thought, his cell phone rang loud and clear, it was Beth. Oh shit.

CHAPTER SEVEN

Another fine morning greeted David, slowly he woke up in his apartment above the shop, to the sound of his cell phone ringing. It's playing *Witchy Woman* by Pop Royals, a specific ringtone for Beth when she calls.

He groggily answered. "Bob's Morgue, you stab 'em, we slab 'em, how can I help you?"

"Lord, are you still in bed? Its 9am." Brianne had obviously borrowed Beth's phone.

"Hey, we have to go out of town, big Witch shindig, that special time of the year, blah blah blah." In the background Beth can be heard.

"Nice and sensitive there, babe. Way to show support for your wife."

"Aw, Honey, I didn't realize you were such a little bitch?"

The retort comes quickly and sharply, "Fag."

Meanwhile, David is trying to figure out why he hasn't hung up yet.

"Sorry to interrupt your intellectual, interpersonal discussion, but is there a point coming?" Brianne snaps back to reality.

"So yeah, um, Beth and I wanna make sure you will be okay and that we will be out of cell range and we won't be able to be contacted for a few days. So, do us a favor, don't take any difficult jobs like Rakshasas or anything, just stay with the shop...oh maybe sell something so Beth feels like she brings something to the table!"

"Fuck you!" Beth fires back.

David starts to laugh, "you have such a loving, warm relationship. Okay, I will stick to the shop, have fun sacrificing animals and burning things!" David hangs up before a vulgar retort can be fired his way.

After getting cleaned up and eating a quick breakfast, David descended to the shop to open it up. David gets so wrapped up in investigations and removals that he forgets there is also a shop for magical support and pursuits. After about an hour and a couple of phone calls which amounted to nothing, change your cell phone plan, etc. A few curious people arrived, a few quiet practitioners who strolled through the shop. Most were lookers, curious, but not buying. Then a few people walked who looked for specific ingredients, items, questions about who selected the inventory. The individuals dressed similar, spoke in a particular cadence. David thought it was odd, but realized it was probably a coven of some kind. He still worked hard to make a mental note of their appearance and of the pendants that they wore. Beth had given him a quick rundown of sigils for various demons, gods and other non-defined, extra-dimensional beings. The sigil pendants were familiar, but he could not place them right away. After they left, he quickly dug for a paper from his desk to draw it, so he could research it later. Nothing the group purchased was particularly foreboding, but who knows what ingredients they already had. It was the questioning that pinged his personal radar. David was sure to be vague about Beth. After that last cult attempted to sacrifice her and leave him as puppy chow for Brianne, he has grown more aware and cautious when people start asking questions. He informed them that he got the ingredients from several outside vendors and researched what he needed online. He told him that, his partner, was just there to help itemize and track sales, she was not into the craft.

Later, while David was doing the inventory to see if Beth needed to purchase, grow or otherwise acquire any replacement items, he turned to find standing before him a young girl, roughly 12 years old in appearance.

"Whoa, I didn't hear you come in." David said almost shrieking out the words.

The girl stood there for a moment, smiled and looked David over, as though she could look into him, to see the kind of person he really was.

Finally, she spoke, "You seem rather awake to the real world, but this part does not seem to be you. Your partner, she is a Witch?" David was now the one standing in silence, studying the girl.

Her look, demeanor, even her word selection seemed unnatural.

"What do you know of Witches?"

The girl smiled, raised an eyebrow and said, "More than you could possibly fathom."

Her eyes, just for a moment, seemed to have a jade light within. David did his best to control his emotions, he didn't wanna tip his hand, but he knew something was very wrong. David needed to get to his desk, get to something to defend himself with. Blessed water, salt, Goofer Dust, wardings, whatever he could grab. He began to slowly turn toward his desk, keeping his eyes upon the girl, when a thump came down upon his head and darkness filled his vision.

Moments later, David awoke. His head was pounding, his vision was blurred. He was still in the shop. A low murmur could be heard coming from the stock and garden room. David moved to the stairs, up to his room. David moved as fast and as well as he could. He slammed his shoulder into his apartment door and moved to a large, locked cabinet. Pulling a key from his pocket, he worked the lock and flung open the doors. This revealed a small arsenal of weapons. David grabbed the tactical shotgun and a box of ammo marked 'kitchen sink.' As he moved back down the stairs, he loaded the weapon and shoved the rest of the rounds into his pockets. David rounded the door leading to the back room. Within the area that Beth had set up a small hydroponic garden, for easy restock, there was a round table standing. Inscriptions of odd, unrecognized symbols adorned the table and the walls around.

The young girl was tied to the table, with chains that had the same symbols etched into them. Four individuals, in bronze hooded cloaks, stood around her and were all murmuring some unrecognizable chant. The same bronze and red cloaks that the freaks who tried to sacrifice Beth wore. This can't be a coincidence, but why the child? As a matter of fact, this is the same setup from last time, just on a smaller scale and how exactly do they have the chains and the paint and everything else? Is there some Supernatural Walmart...one-stop ritual shop? Seriously, do they all go to the same "how too" seminar on how to have a ritual? David mused to himself. Well, this time, I am ready for their shit! David racked a round into the chamber. Immediately everyone in the room was aware of him and looking at him, in a most unhappy fashion.

"Just what in the ever Fuck, are you doing?" They stood there, still staring at David. "That is your cue to talk, before I start shooting."

The nearest figure drew a weapon and screamed "Defiler!" Before the person could take a second step, David did not hesitate to fire. A loud bang, a flash and a searing noise filled the room. The "person" writhed and began to burn. Whoever, whatever they were, they were not entirely human. As David turned his attention back to the rest of them, the leader mumbled something, raised his hand and sent David flying back against the wall while his shotgun warped and bent in the middle, as though it absorbed some great force. The other two figures drew similar, large daggers and moved towards David. He looked at the shotgun, realizing it can fire, turned it immediately into a club. The closest figure felt the smack of the butt of the shotgun and went reeling backward. The second, unfortunately scored a slice upon David's arm. David recoiled back to the wall dropping the shotgun, the figure followed, drawing back for another slice. David plunged his hand into his pocket, drew out a shell, snapped the top off and threw the contents towards the attacker.

When the contents, which were salt, silver and various protective herbs and blessed water hit his face, steam began to rise. The person screamed and fell back to the floor, burning from the exposure. David followed through with a right cross, knocking the person out. David turned to the last figure, the leader and drew out a couple more shells. In all the calamity, he failed to notice until now, how calm the girl was.

"Everything is gonna be okay, I am gonna get you out of this!" David yelled dramatically, like some old movie house cliffhanger episode.

For the first time, the leader spoke...well at least a language

David could understand.

"You will not stop this, you will not interfere, you will just die!" The leader's face seemed to have changed from earlier in the shop.

There was something decidedly not entirely human about his look. His eyes were dark, almost black and large, almost the same as a cow's. His skin seemed very thick, his mouth almost seemed to extend, like a muzzle. David's revulsion read all over his face. His eyes glanced back to the girl; she was still calm. Just then the leader began to chant, louder and more distinct, his eyes began to glow with a blue flame. An energy orb began to form in front of him, David began to look for something to dive behind, having a good idea about what was about to happen. Just as the orb reached full power, the girl muttered something and the orb dispersed. Both the leader and David slowly turned to the girl, both equally shocked and confused.

The girl let out a giggle and spoke, "Well, that was a fun show and I know the climax would have been spectacular, but my favorite little one would have been absolutely heartbroken had I allowed David to be seared to a crisp."

The leader turned his full attention to her.

"Impossible, you couldn't have done that! You are bound, restrained, your powers are voided!"

The girl grinned as wide as the moon, "Oh dear, do mean these markings? Let me guess, you pulled your spells from the Aldract Grimoire?" The leader looked perplexed; how could she have known?

"Funny thing about that book, most don't realize this, but I wrote it. Funny story, spells that I create, I can undo with a thought. Sooooo, I was never really your prisoner or sacrifice, I was just curious about him." The girl shot a look back to David, "My favorite speaks about you a lot David, so I wanted to test you, see what you are really made of."

"Wait, you knew this would happen, you let yourself be taken, just to see what I would do?" David seemed rather annoyed now.

"You should be proud, I don't impress easy, I went into this very skeptical and was proven to be very wrong."

"Just who exactly are you?" David shouted.

"This is the Dark Lord Asmodeus, Lord of the Abyss, General of..." Asmodeus interrupted.

"Oh dear, I forgot you were there, that is enough from you. Tell Moloch, next time face me directly if he has an issue with me, don't send lap dogs." In an instant, the girl shrugged off the bindings, jumped from the table and struck the leader so hard, his head spun around, twice.

After David gathered the bodies into a single pile, Asmodeus walked through the store and gathered ingredients together which would remedy the problem of the remains and leave no trail for anyone to follow. After the deed was done, David sat at his desk, Asmodeus sat across from him.

"So, you're a demon lord?" David asked slowly.

The little girl smiled, "Oh I am, yes indeed and so much more." The girl beamed.

"So, when Beth prays or communes or asks for wisdom, help, whatever ...she is asking you?" David asked.

"You seem confused by this."

"No, no, just I never met someone's deity, or whatever."

"Well, I am not her God, I didn't create her, I guide her, influence her, I help her grow and embrace the powers within her. I sometimes grant her boons, abilities or pieces of wisdom and she appeases me with things I enjoy."

"Don't take this wrong, but I didn't think demons were...helpful?"

The girl smiled, "Yes, most people don't understand. Don't get me wrong, there are demons out there to avoid at all costs. Such as the lovely chap who orchestrated this mess."

"So, Beth is important?" David asked curiously.

"She is special to me, I have many followers to be sure, but she is one of the only ones who can see me as something of a friend or father figure. She works to appease me, without asking for anything in return. I have lived a long time, rarely have I come across someone so devoted who did not have an ulterior motive, one who did not make an attempt to take more than they deserve or have earned. She is remarkable and I value her existence, which means I like to know the people that are close to her. So that takes us back to you and why I needed to test your metal, so to speak. She is too precious to me to have her wasting time on useless or substandard people."

"I am hoping I passed this test?" David sheepishly asked.

"Oh, I like you. The moment your head cleared the first thing you did was seek to intervene on the girl's behalf. You also worked very hard to hide Beth's existence from them, I was listening when they were pumping you for information, they would have come for her as well."

"You heard all that too?"

"I hear a lot of things."

"Well, I am glad I passed the test, but maybe next time we just have dinner if you wanna get to know me?" Asmodeus smiled big again.

"Oh, that sounds like a wonderful idea!" Just then, the little girl apparated and David was once again alone.

David got up, closes the shop door and moved to his apartment and wondered how he would explain any of this to Beth or if he will even have to?

CHAPTER EIGHT

David was sitting at his desk in the office, scrolling through articles on his laptop. Political rhetoric and backlash filled most of each page, followed by economic corruption and celebrity scandals. His eyes were starting to cross as he searched for the right article, with the right combination of words. Beth was not at the office; she was enjoying some downtime. The two have had a slow week, nothing really happened anywhere. David was bored and thinking about lunch, it was around 1pm, when suddenly the office phone rang. David took a second to react, he had almost completely zoned out, staring at articles.

"Good afternoon, Metaphysic Investigations, David speaking how may ...what do you want?" David's professional tone ended upon realizing Beth was giggling on the other end of the line.

"Oh, you sound so official, it's just a privilege to listen to you!"

"Are you so bored you need to bother me on your day off?"

"Actually no, I need you to come to the house, there is something very important I need to show you?"

"Oh yes? Your wife created another expensive, mind-altering video game?"

"No, she already finished her most recent project a couple weeks ago, this is something else, so get your lazy ass up and come to the house."

"Hey, I am extremely busy, one of us has to keep this place afloat, I have calls to manage, ads to pay for, clients to..." Beth cut him off.

"You are so full of cow dung; I can smell it over the phone. Seriously, this is very important and I want you to be a part of this."

"Okay, now I am very intrigued, what is it?"

"It is way easier to show than to explain, so get going."

"Fine, fine...I am on the way."

Their house was about 45 minutes from the office. David grabbed some gear, reflexively and made sure to slam a Mountain Dew, just to ensure full consciousness. The drive was pleasant as always, no one really lives near them, it is just pleasant scenery. David arrived at Beth and Brianne's place. He parked in their large driveway and walked to the front door. The house was reminiscent of an old cabin, rustic, but quaint. As

Shadow Walking

David approached the door, there was a note upon it. Go around back and follow the worn path into the woods, Beth.

What is this, a scavenger hunt, a picnic? David started to grumble, then he thought about the picnic idea and realized he was hungry and his grumbles faded at the hope for readymade food. David walked the path for about 5 minutes when he started to call out, to make sure he was going the right way. A fairly close sounding call came back. 'Over here David.'

A few moments later David rounded a rather large, old oak tree to find Beth standing on the other side with a warm smile upon her face.

"Okay, so here I am, what is the deal are we having a picnic or what, cause I could really eat?" Beth's smile broadened.

"The deal has to do with Brianne, but I think she is the only one that will have a picnic today." David looked confused by that statement.

"What the hell is that supposed to mean?"

"Why don't you ask Brianne, she is right over there."

"Okay crazy lady, so Brianne what...." David turned as he asked for clarification.

Before he could finish the question, standing not far from him was Brianne, but not the human version. Brianne was in full Werewolf mode, growling and frothing.

"Oh, holy shit...holy shit!" David began to run up the path.

Brianne pursued. All Beth could hear was a constant 'Oh shit' coming from David as he ran for his van. She smiled, laughed and then said.

"Hun that is enough, stop teasing him." At that moment, Brianne, who had been easily keeping pace with David, pounced upon him, he was still yelling.

Brianne leaned in as though she was going to tear David's throat, when she gently licked his face. David laid perplexed. Was she checking the flavor first? Brianne then rolled off David onto her feet. There was a gentleness in her eyes as she squatted down near him making a very low rumbling sound, similar to a cat's purr. After a couple minutes Beth caught up to them.

"Surprise!" David still had a confused and a severe WTF look on his face.

He did not say anything yet. Beth read his face and could feel his fear and confusion. Her smile became a little sheepish.

"*Sorry*, if it's any consolation, this was Brianne's idea and I *initially* was against it." The fear was ebbing away from David's face as complete annoyance washed over it.

After a moment of Beth still sheepishly grinning and Brianne now softly whimpering David finally spoke.

"So, what exactly is this, besides a plan to steal several years from my life?" His tone was sarcastic with a touch of pissed off.

Beth cleared her throat, "Remember, Brianne was not in control, the Moon held sway over her changes."

"Yeah, okay." David was still stuck in frustration.

"Okay…well, do you see the Moon?" The tumblers in David's head clicked.

Shadow Walking

It was past 2 pm in the afternoon and Brianne was in full Werewolf mode.

"Holy shit, you found a spell or a potion? David was now noticeably excited; no trace of annoyance or anger was left.

"It was neither, apparently after her last birthday, she awoke the next day with a deeper feeling of connection to the wolf side of her. Apparently, all her work on meditating coupled with my empathic influence pushed the process forward." David looked slightly perplexed again.

"So, this was something that was going to happen anyway?"

"Oh yes, but usually not for several years, providing the person lives that long and actually worked toward control. According to the most recent lore I discovered, most stay under the influence of the Moon because they cannot accept what they have become. This makes the process take longer, but Brianne had embraced this aspect of her life from the first time she changed at 15."

"So, she can change back and forth anytime she wants now, that is the point, yes," David looked a little perplexed again, "So why is she still like this?"

Beth crinkled her face a bit, "because, she doesn't have anything to wear, she is naked under all that fur, genius."

"I don't mind, it won't offend me."

Both ladies tilted their heads at him. Apparently, David was 100% again. The group walked back to the house, where Brianne was able to change back and put on some clothing...much to

David's disappointment.

"I mean, you did make me think you were gonna eat me, a little flash is a small price."

"Jeezus David, are you that hard up?" Beth belted out.

Brianne laughed out loud, "he kinda does have a point, that was pretty fucked up babe."

"Wait, what are we talking about here?"

"Nothing Babe, just teasing you." Brianne walked out of the bedroom still laughing.

"Well, David, if I can't flash you, how about I feed you?" Brianne said leaning on the kitchen counter.

"That would be awesome, I am pretty hungry…life and death moments tend to make me work up an appetite."

Beth rolled her eyes, "oh Lord, are you gonna whine about this forever?"

"For-eh-ver!" David over-enunciated.

Brianne laughed and snorted from the kitchen as she whipped up some cheeseburgers.

"So, this has been an eventful couple of weeks for me. I got to meet your…magic guide, Brianne is now in total control, what else, I wonder? So, what about that Beth, your 'father figure' thinks I am Aces!"

"Obviously Asmodeus' mind has worn from the centuries." Beth said drolly.

"Oh, hilarious, so hilarious. You are just mad cause it took years for you to win him over and I did it in an afternoon."

"Oh lord. Well now you have been brought into the family, so to speak. He has taken an interest in you David, your life will be different."

"It already is different, Beth, I am not too worried."

CHAPTER NINE

The next night the girls were getting ready for a night of celebratory dancing. It had been a long time since the two of them went out and just enjoyed the nightlife. This night was doubly special, it was the first night of the full moon for the month and the first time Brianne could do anything besides run through the forest. They were going to a new club to celebrate. There was a new club that had only opened about 2 months ago and everyone said it was fantastic, everyone, according to David. David was waiting in the girls' living room, with little patience.

"Jeez you two, what the hell is the hold-up, can't you just whammy yourselves ready?" David gruffly threw out.

"I'll give ya a whammy if ya don't shut it, Dick Jacket!" Beth called back. Brianne was doing her eyes.

Shadow Walking

"My, such intellectual conversations you two have." She responded, dripping with sarcasm.

"Hey now, whose side are you on anyway?" Beth shot back.

"Oh Hunny, I am on my side as always...Bitch." A very quick slap came across Brianne's backside, a maneuver that hardly garnered a reaction.

"That kind of behavior is only going to slow this process down, Luv." She cooed at Beth.

Beth simply smiled as she worked her hair in the mirror. A substantial amount of time later, the ladies entered the living room.

"Ta-dah!" Beth exclaimed.

The two were dressed in tight-fitting dresses, that accentuated their curves wonderfully. Brianne was wearing a black and red dress, while Beth had a soft green dress. The two were wearing 4-inch heels, something neither of them wore, almost ever. Beth styled her hair, so it draped and covered the right side of her face, while Brianne wore her hair up, gelled into place. They had a modest amount of makeup on, mostly eye shadow, giving them each a smokey eye look. On their arms, were matching colored purses. David was on the couch and pretended to be asleep.

"Huh, Wa.... what's going on, what year is it?" The two ladies looked unimpressed with his humor and were waiting for a remark on their appearance.

David jumped up, "it is about damn time!" The two were still glaring at him, "what? I got something in my teeth?"

Their collective look was growing sterner.

David began to grow a smirk across his lips, "you two look amazing."

"About time loser!" Brianne fired off.

"I am sorry, I didn't know I was on affirmation patrol today?" David remarked, "while we are on the subject of looks, what about me?"

David had on black dress shoes, with socks to match, dark slacks and a blood-red button-down shirt. His hair was short as usual and no makeup. He was sporting a five o'clock shadow though. The girls looked him over.

"Not bad, I wasn't sure you had nice clothes." Beth joked.

Brianne looked him over, "lookin good Babe!"

David seemed to grow a few inches taller from the admiration.

"Okay, if the mutual appreciation society meeting is over, can we go?" Beth asked.

The group hopped into the VW Bus and headed to the club. The group arrived at the club. It was a small place but had fantastic music and a terrific DJ. The ladies grabbed a small table while David grabbed a few drinks. After a few minutes at the table and some laughs the DJ announced that retro night would be kicking off soon. David's ears perked up.

"Hey, time for me to bust a move! You ladies care to join me?"

"Oh, but of course, kind sir!" Beth proclaimed.

Brianne spoke up, "Lets Do-it!"

Shadow Walking

No sooner had the group stepped onto the dance floor, then the DJ started off with N'Trance's "Stayin Alive." A familiar riff from the Beegees started and immediately David struck his best Travolta finger point and began to shift his hips.

Brianne broke out into the loudest laughs possible, while Beth cried out, "oh no ...no, no, no, no!" As she attempted to flee the dance floor.

Brianne grabbed her and said, "not so fast Darlin, we are dancing!" At this point the ladies grooved with each other, while David did his best to tear up the dance floor around them.

After a few songs, the girls decided to take a rest and David offered to grab a few more drinks.

The two sat leaning into each other. Beth began to think about the past. Her mind wandered to a certain face. She loved to dance, to cut loose, it was spiritual to her. Alicia, Beth had not thought about her in a while. So much had happened, so many dangers had reared up. A deep sense of worry was weighing on her. David is too eager she thought. So much like Alicia. I think I need to rethink our arrangement. While lost in thought, she did not notice Brianne staring at her.

"Where were you Babe? Wherever it is, it doesn't seem good." At that moment Beth snapped out of memories.

"No, I am...I am good ...sorry Hun."

"This is supposed to be fun, Hun. Celebrating, remember?" Brianne smirked.

"I know, I know, I am sorry I don't mean to be broody."

Darren Anderson

"You mean more than normal?" Brianne struck back with.

"Oh, ya know, you are lucky you are sexy!" The two leaned in for a deep kiss and then embraced.

Across the dance floor, David was heading to the bar for more refreshments. As he walked, he noticed a scene developing on the other side. A young lady seemed to be getting harassed by four thug wannabes. These were the type of guys who show up in small-town clubs to try and look hard and intimidating. David scanned the area and noticed the bouncers were all too busy flirting or drinking to be bothered. So, without further thought David darted over to the lady's side. Placing a hand on her shoulder, he pulled her back and stepped forward.

"Yo fucker, whatchu think you doin?"

"What am I doing?" David said with a thick wannabe gangster tone, "I am keeping you from making a mistake, the lady is not interested."

"The Bitch ain't yo prob Cuz!" The main thug was about six foot three, blonde-haired with cornrows.

Difficult to tell his bulk or weight, because of an extra fluffy jacket. His crew wore matching attire, some with sunglasses, some with gold, wife beater shirts all the stereotypical wannabe wardrobe. David snapped back from analyzing his opponents to respond.

"Well, the Bitch may not be, but the lady is." The main thug laughed and pointed to his crew.

"Oh, we got a white knight boyz, what we do bout that?"

Shadow Walking

"Fuck him up!" Was the collective call from his crew.

"Sorry Cuz, this ain't yo night." With that comment the wannabe lunged forward with a wild swing for David's head.

Not nearly as fast as a Wendigo or Rakshasa, David thought. He immediately sidestepped the swing and stepped into the thug with a short uppercut into the thug's ribcage. He let out a loud gasp and groan as he dropped like a wet rag to the ground. His crew was still laughing when he hit the floor. They stopped after a couple seconds with looks of disbelief.

"The fuck you do to Ryan?" They all looked on in disbelief. Like their minds had yet to register what had happened.

"Ryan ...the gang leader is named Ryan?" David thought out loud.

Immediately Princess Bride came to mind, the part about no one fearing The Dread Pirate Wesley. David started to laugh when the other three rushed him. David dived forward taking the legs out of the middleman. His face smacked the floor like a flapjack. He rolled to his side, barely conscious. The other two stumbled into each other trying to turn back around. Again, they charged but David dodged the first and sent a left hook into the other. This sent the thug careening into the wall as David spun around to block a shot from the last one standing. Thug number four threw another shot as his first was blocked and socked David on his temple. David was stunned a bit, but still in the game. The wanna be threw another shot, but David ducked it and came up right under his jaw with a well-placed left. This thug's night was over. David strolled over to the group and appraised the scene. Just as he was getting ready to gloat, a solid club came crashing down on his head from behind. Apparently, the crew had three other members. As David went to the ground, the three cheered, mocked and began to kick. Across the room, at a small table, Beth all at once gleaned what had just happened to David.

Brianne ...David...Help! These three words sent Brianne running from the table. Her ancient bloodline had awoken in her and she began to change. At the same moment Beth began to call upon Asmodeus with a chant for the clouding of minds. A spell that created just enough haze and darkness to obscure Brianne's face from prying eyes. Just as the thugs on the floor started to rise, just as the last three decided that feet were not enough and brought out more weapons, Brianne pounced. In a flash, the first thug's face was pushed nearly through the closest wall. Another arm was grabbed and snapped, like a dry brittle twig. The third met claws across his face and then a returning backhand that sent him through the air. Of the four who were put down first, Ryan rose first only to feel the fury of Brianne.

Her strike to his ribs was much more devastating than David's and several ribs cracked. A swift kick took the next one out at his knee, breaking it cleanly. The third who had been slumped next to the wall was met with a stiff jab that sent him quickly and neatly right back into the same, slumped position. The last, possibly the only smart one had viewed the carnage that took place in a matter of a few seconds decided to run for his life. Not a bad idea, but not thought of fast enough. Brianne casually caught up to his sprint, promptly grabbed him from behind by his shoulders and slammed him to the floor, knocking every bit of wind and consciousness from his body.

As Brianne was taking out the trash, Beth had rushed to David's side to help him recover. A minor incantation and a few gestures had David feeling much better.

"What in the world is wrong with you, what were you thinking?" Beth was uncharacteristically loud and stern. "You can't just go off all halfcocked, getting in fights, risking your life, what is wrong with you? Are drunken brawls your idea of fun?" David's mind was clearing and the riot act being read to him was sinking in and confusing him.

"Whoa, whoa, whoa, slow your roll Captain Careful. The guys were harassing and probably thinking of raping a young girl. No one seemed to care, not the people around her, not the bouncers, not anyone, what was I supposed to do?"

"You call the police or help or something!" Beth remarked.

"And then what, watch it happen, listen to her cry and pretend it's a movie? I hunt monsters and angry spirits, am I supposed to run from thugs?"

"Ya well, maybe that needs to change too." Just then Brianne stepped to Beth's side.

"How are you Babe, feeling better?"

"Those cunts' are toast, FYI." Brianne said with pride. Thanks for the assist, Bri, I was just getting on them."

"Yeah, I know, but I was bored."

Beth interrupted, "hey, this isn't a joking time, this is serious, you almost got really hurt or maybe killed! This is not a game or playtime or." Beth was almost exasperated.

Brianne spoke up, "hey Beth, what is this? It was a bar fight, they happen all the time, David did a good thing."

"He did not do good, he got beat up and for what?"

"Helping a defenseless person?" David added.

David had a perplexed look as the emotion overtook Beth's face. She was positively flummoxed that neither of them could understand how serious and wrong this was. In her mind, she kept seeing Alicia's lifeless body lying where David was just a moment ago. Tears were starting to pool in her eyes. After a moment of silence, David spoke up.

"This is about her, isn't it?" Beth's eyes widened and she went pale, "I have never pushed you about that time in your life, I always figured when you were comfortable you would share the whole thing. It is very apparent that it weighs down on you, your guilt is crushing you and you are projecting that onto me."

Beth started to say something, but David cut her off, "No, I am not done. Look, I am not Alicia, I am not your girlfriend or your kid or your responsibility. I don't fully know what happened, but I can guess something bad happened and for whatever reason you think it's your fault, it went down. I get that, I really do and I am sorry Beth. But I am not Alicia. I make my own choices and I take responsibility for me. You think you made a mistake showing me these things, teaching me about what is out there and letting me take cases. But if you remember, I was at the asylum too, I was there on my own. I already took that path. My grandfather taught me things; he was the one who started me off. You showed me how much more there is? I wouldn't trade this life for anything! Don't you get it? I have seen more than I ever thought possible. My two best friends are an amazing Witch and a fucking Werewolf who can control her change at will! If you think for one minute, I blame you for any danger I encounter, you are out of your mind! Before you, I probably would have walked away, pretended I didn't see her in trouble, safe in my cowardice."

Beth interrupted, "But you got hurt, you got beat!"

"After I kicked the crap out of four and had I not been so pleased with myself, I would have seen the other three and beat them two! Fortunately, I know a badass Werewolf who was ready to rock and roll all over their punk asses!" At which point David and Brianne share a high five.

"Babe, I don't wanna make you feel bad, but David saved a person, he kicked ass and has been doing that for quite a while now, you should be proud." Brianne added.

Beth stood for a few moments, trying to process the situation. She thought about everything that she had seen David do, everything he had handled and still kept a great attitude. She realized he belonged in this world every bit as much as she and Brianne did.

"I am sorry, I just couldn't see past my mistake. I thought I was making the same one all over again."

"Gee thanks, glad you think I am a mistake!" David said with a huge smile upon his face.

"Ya know what I mean dick-jacket!"

"There she is, there is my favorite Witch!" David sarcastically announced. Brianne burst out in another round of loud laughter and snorts.

As the three began to calm down and laugh a bit, the young lady David had saved approached. She walked up to them.

"I just wanted to tell you how awesome that was." David beamed.

"It's okay, I am here to help." A sudden look of confusion came across her face.

"Oh, I mean yah, but I was talking to her." She looked toward Brianne.

Brianne had been looking rather proud toward David when she snapped her eyes toward the girl.

"I am sorry, what did you just say?" Beth and Brianne responded in unison.

The girl, looking a little more sheepish replied, "Well, I mean you did okay I guess, but you girl, you were off the chain!" Before she could continue to gush Brianne cut her off.

"Are you fucking kidding me? You realize this guy; this guy right here was the only one who saw you in danger and acted on it! I didn't come for you or save you; I came to help him! The only reason he even needed help was three more guys came from behind. Three more after he beat four ...that's four...by himself! And he is just okay, just did alright?" At the same moment Beth's eyes had begun to change, her lips started to move subtly.

David saw this and grabbed her, "Hey, hey, I just got my ass kicked saving her, don't make that a vain act by barbecuing her!"

Beth's eyes changed back as she rolled them and sighed, "Fine, I won't." Brianne's tirade was still going on.

The girl was in a state of shock, she wanted to run, but her legs wouldn't work.

"Next time some guy saves you, try and actually appreciate it! Now get your skank ass out of his site!" David sat and watched the whole show.

"Wow, Brianne, that was fantastic!"

"No problem Babe, bitch needs manners!"

David looked at Beth, "Remind me to always stay on her good side!" Beth laughed and nodded. The three of them exited the club and went back to the gals' place to finish celebrating life.

CHAPTER TEN

The following week, Brianne had successfully debugged a new game for a large game franchise. This was a major contract and major success. Not only was Brianne able to find and debug an issue no one else could seem to find, but she did it on schedule. The entire corporate office believed it would never happen on time and that the release was going to have to be pushed way back. This was gonna cost the corporation, not to mention it would anger fans everywhere. So being the hero of the day earned her a great paycheck, plus a nice bonus, tacked on. This was how appreciation was shown in the corporate world. So, to celebrate her success as well as recent changes in their lives, Brianne decided that the office should close and all three friends should spend a week in Vegas!

Shadow Walking

"While I appreciate the invitation, wouldn't you two rather celebrate alone?" He had a half-smile on his face, "I mean, don't you two wanna...*celebrate*?" David was making awkward hand gestures to go along with not so subtle implications.

David was leaning on his desk, within their office. Beth was checking over her inventory at that moment. She stopped in front of a shelf and looked up and tilted her head.

"I am sorry, what are you trying to say?" Beth squinted at David. "I mean, you know, a little back and forth or drawing the curtains or..." Beth cut David off. "I think you should stop talking. Look, Brianne wants her closest family with her. The other stuff will happen when you are in your own room."

"What? I thought we were bunking together? I wanted you to read me bedtime stories!"

"You are a jackass."

"So wait, I am family?"

Beth walked around from the shelves, "Are you kidding me? You have to ask?"

"Well, I mean, I never really was close to anyone, besides my Grandpa." David was getting red in the face.

Beth's frank tone hit home. The two of them considered him family, truly. Beth could see the emotion rise in him.

"Oh God, you aren't gonna cry or anything. Are you?"

"Nooo. I don't do that." David took a deep sniff to hold himself back a bit.

"So, you don't think of us as a family?" Beth asked, with an eyebrow raised.

David went from elation to slight terror at the question. He had never really thought about it. But, after a second, he realized they were closer to him than anyone ever had been, save for his Grandpa. He knew them, their secrets, their past and who they were now. Beth was still waiting for a response.

"You okay David, did you have a stroke?" David realized he had been standing there for a few moments with a blank expression.

"Sorry, I got lost realizing… I mean, I realized, yeah you two are family." Now Beth's face softened, her eyes welled a bit.

David smiled, "Aww are you gonna cry?"

Beth's face went very stern again, "Don't make me hurt you."

The next day, David showed up at Beth and Brianne's house. They decided not to road trip it this time. They didn't wanna waste a single day of the trip on driving. So, David was there to drive them all to the airport. An hour later, David was parking in the extended-stay lot. When they unloaded their luggage, David locked up the Bus and stood for a moment and looked at it. Beth turned back and asked if they needed a moment alone?

"Funny lady, really funny."

The three boarded the flight and were shown to the first-class seating.

"Wow, Brianne, top-notch all the way!"

"Hey if you are gonna splurge, do it right!"

The chairs were large and comfortable. The lovers were

Shadow Walking

seated together, with Brianne at the window seat. David was located across the aisle from them. The jet started its path down the runway. As it accelerated, Beth sunk into her seat. She had never flown before and was a little nervous. David was excited, he had flown a few times, but it had been a few years. Brianne had plastered her face to the window. She had also never flown, but absolutely enthralled by the experience.

As they gained altitude, Brianne called for Beth, "look! Babe, look, look! Everything is so small!"

"Uh-huh, that's great." Upon hearing the tone, Brianne turned back to her.

"I'm sorry Babe, is this rough for you?"

"A little, but I am doing okay. Maybe we should get a drink?" Maybe I could get 10, Beth thought to herself.

"Yeah, a drink hun, let's get a drink." The attendant had started her way down the aisle.

The seat belt sign was off and David had jumped up and leaned over Beth to look out the window.

"Awesome! Colorado looks so amazing from this altitude!"

Brianne kicked in with an, "I know, right?"

Beth had rolled her eyes into the top of her head. These two, Jeezus.

"Okay the alcohol is near, return to your seat."

David looked at Beth. "What?"

"Move, Monkey Boy, I need booze and I need it now!"

"Whoa there alchy, you will get your fix!"

"Don't make me test the foot-pounds required to open that emergency door!"

David recoiled back to his seat and looked the attendant in the eye, "Whatever you give, make it a double."

The attendant smiled and giggled a bit, "lots of people get nervous when they fly, but it really is safe." She assured Beth.

"Yah, yah, a jack and coke please." Beth said in a curt fashion.

Several drinks and a short nap later the group landed in Vegas.

"That wasn't that bad, right Babe?" Brianne asked Beth.

"So long as the booze didn't run out, it was great."

David went ahead to collect their bags, so the gals could hit the bathroom and recoup a bit. As the gals got to the baggage claim they found David standing there with all of the bags. "As luck would have it, our bags also planned a Vegas trip!" David mused.

The trio grabbed their gear and moved outside the terminal to catch an Uber. After a short trip, they arrived at their hotel. Brienna had booked a couple suites at the Luxor Hotel. The ladies took one room and David grabbed the one next door.

"Hey, there is an adjoining door, we should open it and have sleepovers and stuff, make it one big room, like super stylish camping!"

"Oh My God, that is so not gonna happen!" Beth smiled wide and tilted her head slightly, Brianne laughed so hard she snorted.

"That hurts my feelings." David was standing in their

doorway now.

"Since when did feelings return to your head?" David adopted a pouty/annoyed face.

Beth turned, saw his face and said, "aww" and slammed the door!

She heard a muffled, "I don't like either of you," come from the hallway.

Beth texted David's phone. 'Be ready in a couple hours to start the fun.' The reply was quick, 'I will be ready and I still don't like you.' Beth smirked at her phone and set it down. Brianne was already in the shower.

"Hey babe, I think we really could use this trip," she shouted from the bathroom, "what do you think?"

Just then the glass door opened and Beth stepped in with her. Wrapping her arms around her.

Beth told her, "Oh yes, we all needed this trip. I love you so much for this and so much more. You, me, and David, we have gone through a lot in such a short span."

Brianne had turned at this point and was looking into Beth's eyes.

"We survive, we grow and we become more than just the sum of our experiences. That is what life is Babe!" The two gazed for a moment and then moved in for a kiss.

As the steam rose, the strength of their embrace also rose. They moved in sync with one another. Hands touching, caressing, loving each other. Brianne slid down Beth's body and explored every inch with her mouth. David was scanning through the multiple channels of HBO that were free with the room when a loud, yet muffled cry came out of nowhere. After a couple seconds, the tumblers clicked and David realized what was happening. He smiled slightly to himself. Then the smile faded a bit as he pondered how lonely he was. I really need a girlfriend.

After a few hours, David was knocking at their door. After a moment the door opened. Beth was standing in a tight green dress, which hugged her curves in the best possible way. David was in black slacks with a purple Polo shirt.

"Well aren't you looking spiffy?"

"And you are looking amazing yourself!" David was quite sincere.

He had never seen Beth dressed quite this well before, it caught him off guard a bit. Amazing makeup, hair styled differently. Way more effort than that night at the club.

"So, um." David was still struck by her look and took another moment to refocus his thoughts.

"Uh, so yeah, you two have a little fun while getting ready?"

Beth scowled a bit, "what do you mean?"

Just then Brianne popped out of the Bedroom of the suite and said, "Oh yeah, shower sex is awesome!"

Beth's eyes popped a bit and she slightly blushed.

"Brianne!" She yelled; her voice almost cracked like a boy hitting puberty.

Shadow Walking

"What? Like he couldn't hear us? He is right next door." Brianne was wearing an equally form-hugging deep purple dress.

The dress accentuated her muscular and toned form.

"Since when are you all of a sudden a prude, babe?"

David started to laugh, "Back to being my Mom again, huh Beth? Shield me from the violence, the danger and that Mommy and Daddy have sex? Wait, should it be Mommy and Mommy?" Beth's scowl intensity had grown.

She did still think of David as her ward, her child almost. She did still feel responsible for him and slightly embarrassed that a more intimate part of her life had been put on glaring display. Brianne was now next to David, leaning on him.

"That is a beautiful shade of red babe, but I don't think it goes with the dress."

"Okay, the gang up on Beth part of the day is at a close. Can we just move on to the celebration portion of the night?" The two were smiling wide, like a Cheshire Cat!

They looked at each other, squinted for a moment, looked back and said "sure." The group moved to the casino floor. Beth's eyes beamed at the sight of the slots. So many lights and colors! Brianne was watching her.

"So, where do we start? We do get to play a bit?" Beth sheepishly asked.

"Of course!" Brianne held up a wad of twenty-dollar bills.

"Lets' go to town," David was digging out his wallet, "time

to make Daddy rich!" David said a swarthy tone.

The two ladies had just sat down and upon hearing him, swiveled in their chairs to look at him.

"Aren't you already rich?"

"It's a figure of speech. Come on, we are in Vegas! Gotta capture the vibe right?"

The two squinted and swiveled back around. David sat down at a machine near them and all began to play. Just then a cocktail waitress came by. She had on a shiny bronze shirt with a matching mini skirt, with a red name tag.

"Any drinks?"

"Oh, yes, please!" The waitress took their orders and marched off.

Beth watched her walk away and took notice of the other waitresses and people working. The color was reminiscent of ancient Egypt, but she thought the Luxor had dropped the Egyptian theme? *A resurgence maybe?* Just then Brianne hit the jackpot and all focus was drawn to the machine!

"Hot Damn Babe! I hit!! On a Max Bet, I hit!" The lights flashed, the sound effects fired off and the reels began to spin for her free games.

Beth and David were cheering her on, when the waitress returned with their first round of drinks. Brianne cashed out and moved to another machine. Beth and David followed, hoping some of her luck may rub off. No sooner had they sat down at a new bank of games then another waitress was there to take their orders again. In record time, she returned. Once again, Brianne hit a bonus game. This time, she hit a mid-range progressive and was up to six thousand dollars. Brianne continued her streak and even David and Beth were hitting a stride.

"I can't believe the luck I am having ...is it warm in here?" Suddenly the three began to notice the world was, in fact, fuzzy and warm.

They started to rise and then dropped rapidly to the floor. Casino workers stopped and walked over. They picked up Beth and Brianne while leaving David slumped on the floor, next to his slot machine.

Approximately three hours went by and David groggily sat up on the floor. Countless people walked by, not paying any attention. David looked at himself. His shirt had a couple footprints on it. Apparently, the people not only walked over him, but they also walked on him. Just as he realized this, a person walked by and hit him in the head with a large purse.

"Hey, watch it, lady!" The lady never broke her stride, as though David did not exist.

David finally got to his feet and attempted to interact with the people passing by. Not one person saw him or responded to him. Even the cocktail waitresses paid no attention. David sat back down at the slot machine and slumped over the game. His head was throbbing now, whatever they dosed all of them with was wearing off and had nasty side effects. Where are the girls, were they taken? What the hell is going on? David was trying to remember everything that happened. I tried to remember anything suspicious. Anything that would give him a clue as to what happened. The pain made it almost impossible to focus. David tried to clear his eyes and focus. His gaze was centered on the digital board for the slot machine. it was lighting up in a specific pattern but did not look like gameplay. David squinted and focused harder. The lights came clear. They were spelling something out repeatedly. One word, his name. David. He stared long and hard. Repeatedly he read his own name spell out across the screen. Was this real? David wondered. Finally, he said 'Hello.'

"Hi David, welcome back to clarity."

David read the words and wondered if he was still feeling the effect of whatever had been in his drink.

"I assure you David, this is not a delusion or your imagination. I am talking to you." David could only stare and muster the word 'okay.'

"David, this is Beth's ...special friend, Mr. A." David was still fighting the grog and the pain.

"Mr. A? I don't think I get it."

A.S.M.O.D.E.U.S. As the name spelled out, David's eyes widened.

"Okay, hi there. Listen David, Moloch's minions have the girls. He is planning to do something awful to them. He wants to get to me and will use them to do it."

"What can I do?"

Shadow Walking

"That is an excellent question, David. I need you to say yes."

"Yes to what?"

"I need you to let me in."

"In what?"

"You David, in you." David stared at the words on the screen.

"Hello? David? We don't have a lot of time."

"Are you asking to possess me?" And he is finally on the same page.

"Yes, David, I need your body."

"Wait, you manifested a form last time, can't you just do that again?"

"I could, but it would take time and more power than I want to use right now."

"Is it gonna hurt?"

"David, I will make this quick. Say yes, it won't hurt, you won't feel it, you will just sorta fall into a dream. Please, David, we don't have time."

"Okay, yes, I uh, yes."

"Good boy."

David stood up, he looked around and marveled, "I do so love Vegas."

David looked down at himself. He moved his hands around his whole body.

"My David, you do stay fairly fit. Oh, but this wardrobe, no, no, no." Asmodeus was not impressed with David's sense of style.

"I think there is enough time for a fashion change." As he walked toward the in-house suit shop, he stopped by a Mega-Bucks slot machine.

Asmodeus pulled a twenty from David's pocket. He put it in the machine and hit the spin button.

"Oh, I think that is enough." Asmodeus tapped the machine and the wheels stopped on the major win.

Huge alarms went off and everyone stopped and stared and clapped. A few minutes later attendants were all around him taking information and verifying the hit. Mr. A had just won fifty thousand dollars. He had them take out the taxes and put it on his, meaning David's room account and signed for a special card to access the money. Asmodeus then proceeded to the clothing shop.

Atop the Luxor hotel the ladies were tied to a familiar set of tables. A ritual that had been seen too many times, especially by Beth. They both open their eyes and begin to scan the room.

"Oh Hun, my head is pounding. Brianne, can you change? We are in a bad place and we need to get out of here, quick!"

"I can't seem to, it's like I am blocked."

"What about you babe, can you work anything?"

"No, my head is fuzzy, I can't focus and I feel sick. We got hammered big time. I think I know by who. This setup is familiar."

"Ya gotta be kidding me, Moloch's group again? Why do they seem to have such a hard-on for us?"

Shadow Walking

"Its Asmodeus, they want him. I guess they figure we can draw him out? Wait, where is David? Brianne, do remember seeing David?"

"I don't, but I can't see him or smell him anywhere around. I think they left him behind. I am guessing they didn't see a point to him."

"Last time they left him as a snack for you, he is probably back on the casino floor. Do you think you can maybe reach out to him, Beth?"

"I will really try; in the meantime you should see if you can slip your bonds before someone comes back."

"Too late ladies, we never left." A voice echoed from around a corner.

A large man, in a bronze robe with red trim stepped into the light. He, like the last priest, looked odd. He had an almost bovine look to his face.

"Wonderful, another Moloch piss-boy."

"You would be wise to mind your tongue, witch!"

"What, are you gonna kill us twice? Go screw yourself, heifer." Beth spoke with an indignant tone.

"Our Lord will have you as a sacrifice and then, when Asmodeus surfaces, Moloch will fell him and this will allow him to usurp Asmodeus' power and position. Enjoy what time you have left."

Back at the clothing store, Asmodeus is trying to find an appropriate suit for the night. A lovely young lady approached

- 126 -

him.

"Is there anything I can help you with sir?"

"Oh yes, I need a new wardrobe," David's eyes were uncharacteristically green and seemed to almost glow, "I would like something fitted to me as best as possible and I don't have a lot of time, but money is not an object."

"Come into this room sir and I will see what I can do." The young lady began to take measurements.

When she got to the inseam, there was some hesitation. The brilliance in Asmodeus' eyes grew stronger. The beautiful woman's hands began to shake, she could hardly hold the tape measure. She began to perspire. Her head became filled with lewd thoughts. All she could imagine was taking the man's member into her hands. She didn't even realize she had stopped what she was doing and was staring right at it. All at once her spell broke and she immediately looked up into his eyes.

"Well, dear, it's not going to take care of itself." Her eyes widened and she immediately undid his pants and pulled them down.

Within moments she was enjoying every inch of him. The interlude lasted thirty minutes after the women collected herself and pulled together a wardrobe that suited his needs. It was a bright green and black suit. It was form-fitting yet allowed for quite a range of movement. Asmodeus paid with the hotel card and added quite a bit for the young ladies' time as a tip. As he stepped out of the store, he heard the thumping bass of a night club just across the casino from him. He looked at his newly purchased watch and decided he still had time.

"Ah Moloch, such a slave to tradition and ritual, you will wait until the 19th planetary hour, won't you."

"So, I have a bit of time to kill." He turned his head towards the pounding bass beat, the dance floor called.

Beth and Brianne were still bound, their capturers were preparing for a rather intricate ceremony of some type. Convinced the sigils upon their bindings will keep them out of mischief, they have neglected to check back on them.

"Brianne, are you able to muster anything?"

"Sorry Babe, I am still neutered, it's like I am still drugged, but without the foggy mind. I just can't seem to muster any strength or start to change. It's almost like I am not a werewolf."

"What about you, Babe? Can you work any mojo?"

"I can't, I recited a few spells, but they fizzle and short out. These bindings are good, way better than the last time they restrained me. I think I have something though."

"What is it? Brianne asked. "I can still feel the astral plane. I can still investigate it. The bindings are preventing any of our magic, but I can still reach out."

"Is that gonna accomplish anything?"

"It might, if I can reach someone, someone that can help?"

"You mean Asmodeus?"

"No, pretty sure he is well aware of this situation and is figuring out a game plan. Thing is, we can't afford to wait, I am guessing they are waiting for a particular time or astronomical alignment before they do the deed, but I can't guarantee that, so if it goes too long, they may just cut their losses in case Asmodeus tries to wait them out."

"Do what you can Beth, reach out! Is there anything I can do?"

"Hope and pray."

Asmodeus stepped out onto the dance floor. A deep techno beat was nearly shaking the walls apart. So, this is what the kids like? Asmodeus began to move to the rhythm, slowly at first, then faster. His grace and speed on the dance floor was amazing to behold, people were taking notice, mostly the ladies. Slowly but surely various women began to match, as best as they could, his dance moves. Ladies stopped in mid-conversation, others set their drinks down and moved to the floor. In a short time, Asmodeus had quite the dance troupe behind him. Sprinkled amidst the ladies were a few young men, equally mesmerized by the display. The rest of the men and a few women were in awe at the number of ladies that have swarmed around him.

As the song went on the ladies were getting worked into a frenzy, especially the ones closest to Asmodeus. It began to look more like a clothed orgy than dance moves. The climax, in more ways than one, was hit and the song ended. The group had snapped back to reality and moved back to their tables and seats. Asmodeus laughed and said that it was fun, but I feel the time is almost up.

After nearly an hour, Beth was tired. She reached out into the depths of the Astral Plane, but it seemed to be in vain. Asmodeus was not responding and no one else seemed to be around. She could not even sense David. She struggled to push out the thought that David might be dead. She couldn't do that right now, she couldn't walk that path, Brianne needed her, she needed herself. Suddenly a sweet voice arose from the ether.

"Fine mess sweetie, I thought you were smarter than this?"

"While I appreciate the playfulness, I need real help, if you can't or won't, get off the line, I am busy."

"Wow, that's snarky. I don't remember you being this mean."

"First, my life and the life of my wife is on the line, second, who the hell are you that you know anything about me?"

"Ouch, sweetie, that hurt a bit. I guess it's been a while. In fact, ...Wife? It has been a while."

"Look, I need at least one damn binding removed or damaged, the sigil part, break it and I am home free. Then we can play who we used to be."

The chanting from the other room was louder and stronger. The sacrifice they planned is moments away.

"Please, whoever you are, if you can help, do it now! We are out of time!"

"Easy sunshine, I got you." A focused light appeared and seared one of the sigils off the binding on Beth's right hand.

"Yes! Thank you whoever you are!"

"Ya know, I kinda figured you would know me by now, sweetie." As Beth ripped out of the binding, she turned, her face

Darren Anderson

went pale.

"Sweetie? Alicia?"

"There you go, Beth, I have missed you so." At that moment a partial form manifested.

It was faint and wispy, yet all too familiar to Beth. Her hand came in front of her mouth!

"I looked so hard for you!"

"I know you did baby, but I was far. I just got back to where I could sense you. I struggled so long, I was lost and terrified. But I don't blame you. I did this to myself."

"Alicia, I am so sorry, I should have…"

"Beth stop. Let that go. I love you; I will always love you and I wish you well. Now save your wife!"

"Wait…how, how did you get back?"

"A soft green light found me a while back, it led me back to you. Now go, be safe!" The form disappeared.

Beth was still on the table, staring at the place Alicia had been.

"Beth! Yo Babe, come back!" The shrill voice of Brianne's panic snapped her back into reality.

She turned toward Brianne and muttered an incantation, immediately all of Brianne's and Beth's bindings burned away. At that moment Brianne started to change. The silence had grabbed their attention. No chants could be heard. The group was moving toward them. As the group moved through the doorway, they were welcomed by an unwanted surprise. Brianne was in full form and quite angry. Beth was just behind her, legs folded, hair of green flame and eyes of alabaster. The priest looked toward them with deep hatred in his eyes.

"Defilers! Slaughter them!" Before the first member could take another step, Brianne pounced.

The scream was loud, but quick. Another follower raised a silver blade, but as it swung toward Brianne it began to melt into the follower's hand. His scream was louder and lasted quite a while. The priest stepped forward to engage Beth. His eyes went black and bronze arrows formed before him in the air and launched toward Beth. When they reached a couple feet a shield revealed itself and the arrows shattered upon it. Another follower struck Brianne with a silver dagger, the wound burned almost as intense as Brianne's eyes as she swung back on him and removed his head from his shoulders. A few of the followers moved to back up the priest. They brought out powders and herbs and attempted to disrupt her shield as the priest continued his attack. Amidst the chaos of the confrontation, with Brianne tearing through followers and Beth holding back the priest and setting his assistants a flame, a man walked in. He strolled through the calamity as someone would through a serene park.

"All of this foreplay, is it really necessary? What did it really accomplish, besides dropping the number of followers you have, Moloch." Asmodeus was staring at a corner of the larger room that seemed unoccupied.

"You do realize, I can in fact, see you?" At that moment a form appeared.

Darren Anderson

It stood like a human, two-legged, one head and a couple of arms. That is where the comparison ends. The form was somewhat minotaur like. A very bronze minotaur, but one, nonetheless. It was immense, easily eight feet in height and eyes were of flame. "This is how you come to me, in this pathetic form? A frail human form? I have come for you, for your power and your position! You do not deserve it, not you, not your pathetic brother!"

"Oh, I think you wanna leave Azazel out of this discussion. You think my wrath is awful, Azazel will not talk or play games, he will simply make a decisive, tactical strike, before you even know he is there. Stick to shit talking me. "Face me and fall, sub-creature!" Moloch cried out. A bronze ax appeared within Molochs cloven hands as he charged Asmodeus.

Fire poured from his eyes and his mouth. A lightning-quick swing of the ax nearly sliced Asmodeus' face. His speed was greater though.

"Sub-creature? Honestly, who talks like anymore? The millennium has rolled Moloch, can you at least try to get with the times?" The beast bellowed back and unleashed a stream of flame from his gaping maw.

Asmodeus was engulfed. "Victory!"

"I have burned you from existence!" Moloch roared with pride!

"I thought you could handle more than that. So, your reputation was unwarranted!" Moloch mocked. "Um, who are talking about?" The call came from over Moloch's shoulder, "Seriously? You thought it would be a swing of an ax and a spit of fire for it to be game over?" As Moloch turned, Asmodeus rose, he had slipped something shiny onto his right hand.

He struck Moloch across his face. The blow sent Moloch reeling and the spot where the item touched melted away a part of his face.

Brianne was finishing up the last of the straggling followers. The fight really seemed to bring out the best in her. The stress from everything lately had melted away. She was tired but smiling. Brianne noticed David squaring off with Moloch. She stood there, stunned. She did not know Asmodeus was running the show. It was down to Beth, the priest and a couple of lackeys. The Priest's strength was wavering, he continued to launch anything he could to break her shield, Beth continued to stand fast and pick off his assistants. The Priest was mustering everything he had. A blast of mystic fire that was going to blow a hole in the hotel. The priest sacrificed the two men left, to take the energy of their soul and fortify his attack. Beth could feel the power brewing, she knew her shield would not handle that level of assault, especially after the amount of time she has already had it up and what it has already repelled. She struggled to hold focus and figure out a plan. There was little time, the blast was coming. As the blast emerged, Beth dropped her shield.

The Priest thought he had won! She knows she cannot stop the power. The look of triumphant elation was short-lived. Beth dropped the shield because she needed the focus and energy. She could not repel the blast or stop it, so she moved, moved right into the Priest's spot and subsequently him into hers. She had to wait until the last possible moment, or he could do something, deflect, interfere with a spell, anything. So, as he delighted in what he thought was her end, he shifted space to end up right in front of the force he discharged. The blast incinerated him and blew out a portion of the wall behind him. Beth looked for Brianne and she found her standing, back in human form in the larger room. She was staring at the fight that was still ongoing.

"Brianne, what in the world are you doing? Are you okay, are you hurt?" Brianne did not respond, she slightly tilted her head and pointed to the fray, specifically at David.

"What in the hell?" Beth was almost as shocked as Brianne, till she focused a bit a denoted a particular aura. Asmodeus was in there.

Moloch was furious, his attack became less focused but more intense. He managed to land part of a swing and sliced through David's coat and his left shoulder.

"Well, that was unpleasant." He pulled a cloth from his pocket and dabbed the blood.

Asmodeus turned a clever eye toward Moloch and shoved the kerchief back into his pocket.

"Tell me something Moloch, have you seen this trick? Now you see me, now you don't," The lights dropped from the room and then arose again, "and now you see me everywhere!" As the lights rose, there were a dozen David's standing around Moloch.

An old trick, an old illusion. Moloch had seen this parlor trick before. He swung wide and deep through three of them in a quick moment. The images dispelled.

Asmodeus laughed, "At this rate, you might actually find me!" The nine remaining David's began to move and avoid his hits.

Moloch blasted fire and swung for the fences. Asmodeus avoided every blow, rather all of them did. Over and over Moloch attempted to strike and again and again he failed to hit even one. Asmodeus continued to mock him at every turn.

"Would it help if I produced a red cape for you to aim at? Is it grazing time, do you need a snack? I hear the garden for the casino is quite nice!" Moloch became more incensed, he finally managed to spring forward and catch two more with one strike.

He then turned his head and unleashed a cone of fire that engulfed two more. Moloch was tiring though, the endless streams of fire, the power he granted his servants, the shielding spells and warding to hide his plan. The endless swings of the ax. Not to mention all of his followers were dead and with them their worship, which equates power. Moloch tried to calm himself, at this rate you will burn out, he thought to himself. Wait, the strike, the hit, I bled him. He can't hide that! Catch the scent of human blood and that will be the one to crush! Moloch continued to charge but did not swing hard at all. As he moved past each David copy, he sniffed for blood. Moloch caught the scent, he shifted and moved. He tried not to give away that he had zeroed in. He kept his movements random, moving around the room as though it was still his goal to crush every copy. I have him, he thought. I just need to circle round a little more and I can crush him once and for all! Moloch approached his target. He then turned fainting to go for another version. As he raised his ax he stepped back and swung round rapidly and caught Asmodeus square in the chest! The smile dropped from his face.

Asmodeus looked down at the ax, his eyes were wide. A look of disbelief filled his face. Then an unholy scream escaped his throat! It shook the room. Beth could not believe what she saw. She echoed Asmodeus's scream. Brianne had to grab her or she would surely have attacked Moloch barehanded. Asmodeus erupted with green fluids, his form began to bubble and froth. Moloch dropped his ax, took in a deep breath and unleashed the largest blast of hellfire he could. There was hardly even any ash. The other versions of David began to fade. Moloch raised his arms triumphantly.

"Mine, the power, the position, the armies! I claim them!" Suddenly Moloch stopped.

He had said the word. Power. He did not feel any more power. At his demise, Moloch should have been able to draw off Asmodeus' power as he died. Just then, the sound of his ax scraping the floor as it was lifted was heard. Before Moloch could turn towards the sound, his own ax was plunged deep into his back. Moloch's cry was so terrible it completely overshadowed

Asmodeus'. To lose when he was so close, to have had Asmodeus on the ropes, only to be tricked at the end. But how, how was he undone?

"I imagine you are wondering how this happened?" Asmodeus pulled the kerchief from his pocket again, "that slice you made gave me a wonderful idea. To distort the source of the blood, to transmit it to one of my doppelgangers. I knew eventually you would cue in on the blood."

"Although, it took a lot longer than I thought it would. Little slow there, Bossy!" Moloch struggled and writhed to get the ax out of his back.

Asmodeus, grabbed the handle again and worked it around, turning Moloch left and then right. His pain was immense.

"It is bad enough that you came for me, you bovine parasite, but you came for my favorite and her family. That was rude. I had contemplated letting you crawl back to your pit before it got so ugly. Now, I think I am done with you." With that, Asmodeus ripped the ax from Moloch's back and swung it hard.

The slice went right below Moloch's chin and severed his head cleanly. The lack of any other background noise allowed for an eerily loud thud, when Moloch's head hit the floor.

Brianne and Beth were still dumbfounded. They were still trying to process what had happened when Asmodeus walked up to them.

"So how are you, little one? Quite the holiday, wouldn't you say?"

"I think that rates an understatement award. I have...we have a weird life. I don't regret it, but days like this are a little taxing." Beth softly muttered.

"I know child, I know. It's the burden of being popular." Beth looked down, but also rolled her eyes.

"Now, now child, indignation towards me is not warranted. I had everything in hand."

"Really, which parts? The part where we get drugged and kidnapped, the part where we almost die and have to fight for our lives?"

"Actually Babe, I really didn't mind the fight. I actually feel really good."

Asmodeus smiled, "really? Brianne? You wanna sign off on this?"

"I mean, no, but I can't help but acknowledge that I feel great. I mean aside from when I thought David got killed. Oh, I almost forgot the part about David being taken over and used as a meat wagon!" Asmodeus' face grew stern.

"I did not take anything. I asked him and he agreed." Beth's anger dropped a few notches when she looked at the disappointment on his face.

"I realize that because of my nature, many times it seems I am flying by the seat of my pants. Realize that it is a choice in how I want to live, it is not meant to imply I never have a plan. Now that the deed is done and the danger is over, isn't there anything else you wanted to ask?" Beth looked him in the eyes and paused for a moment.

Then she remembered, "Alicia! Was it you? Did you find her and lead her back?"

"It took a long-time child; I wasn't sure I would ever be able to. Honestly, I got lucky. But yes, the little green light, was of course me."

"Why hasn't she moved on?"

"She did not want to. Not until she had a moment to reconnect to you and make you understand it was not your fault. That she valued your time together and everything you showed her. You need to let the memory of your failure go. You need to truly move on, child."

"Why didn't you ever tell me you were looking for her?"

"As I said, I got lucky. I did not want you to get your hopes up, especially if I could not deliver. So, I kept it to myself."

Brianne wanted to ask something but wasn't sure how to do it.

Asmodeus read her face, "something on your mind, Brianne?"

"Well, I mean, David, is David okay?"

"David is perfectly fine. He is trapped in a fantasy he designed. He is completely unaware of what has happened. Feel free to fill him in, when he gets back."

"And when exactly will we be getting our friend back?"

"My dear child, I have just crushed a would-be usurper, I am exhausted and I think I have earned the right to pamper myself as a reward! Do not worry, you will have him back by tomorrow. In the meantime, feel free to go about the casino and enjoy, I think you may have some good luck tonight!" With that, Asmodeus exited the room.

As he walked out, some men in all black attire carrying all manner of cleaning equipment and bags started to funnel in. As Asmodeus passed the first man, he handed him a stack of something, perhaps chips, they were rather shiny. The man tipped his hat to Asmodeus and he and his crew immediately went to work cleaning the site.

"I guess he actually does make plans, huh Babe?"

The next morning the girls awoke to the sound of someone pounding on their door. It was rather frantic and loud. Beth rose first and staggered to the door. The girls had definitely had some fun last night. Some serious success at the slots and gaming tables as well as plenty of dancing and other frivolities. Beth opened the door to find David standing before her, with only a small towel between him and Beth knowing him on a new level! David pushed through the doorway and sat at the first chair. Beth blinked a few times, trying to process the moment and shut the door.

"Have a good night, did you David?"

"Who is it Babe?" Brianne called out from the bedroom.

"It's a naked David."

"Woohoo, alright David!" Brianne cheered!

"Look, I just woke up about 20 minutes ago! I was naked, no

wallet, no room key, no pants! What the hell happened?"

"It's a long story. How about we get you a new key, get you cleaned up and then some breakfast. I think we have all earned a day to just relax." Beth thought about her life.

Everything she had been through over the years had prepared her what happened. All those moments with Brianne, David, Asmodeus and even Alicia. Everything had come full circle. She realized her life would never be average or normal and that was just wonderful.

Made in the USA
San Bernardino, CA
11 January 2020